Praise for *Libby of High Hopes*

"*Libby of High Hopes* is the sort of book you can't wait to share with someone else because you loved it so much. With fresh, clear prose, charming illustrations, and an absolutely unforgettable heroine, Elise Primavera perfectly captures that moment in childhood when everything seems possible—and impossible—all at the same time. There is a sweetness and an authenticity about this story that's rare and immensely refreshing; it reminded me of the best of Beverly Cleary. *Libby of High Hopes* will keep you nailed to your chair till you turn that final page with a lump in your throat. And don't be surprised if a lot of young readers suddenly start asking for riding lessons. From page one to the last *Libby of High Hopes* is a page turning ride."
    —Diane Stanley

"Elise Primavera has created a young girl with family and friends so real you want to know them all. The journey through her summer is filled with soul and charm, simply wonderful."
    —Petra Mathers

"I wish I could take riding lessons at High Hopes Horse Farm with a friend just like Libby Thump. I was a lot like Libby Thump, always drawing horses and dreaming of riding them. If I'd known her when I was a kid, I'm sure we would have been best friends!"
    —Marissa Moss, author of *Amelia's Notebook*

"A fresh story with some good life lessons and well-developed characters (including the horses). We hope that Primavera will give us more about Libby very soon."
    —Kidsreads.com

"Expressive full-page illustrations appear throughout. The well-written story teaches a gentle lesson that life can be unfair, but persistence and passion payoff."
    —*School Library Journal*

"A solid choice for horse lovers ready to move past early chapter books."
    —*Kirkus Reviews*

"The wide-spaced lines of type and vivid black-and-white drawings make this an accessible, attractive choice for younger chapter-book readers. Primavera offers a nuanced story that acknowledges some of the painful parts of childhood without letting them diminish Libby's resilient nature."
    —*Booklist*

LIBBY of HIGH HOPES

· STORY AND PICTURES BY ·
ELISE PRIMAVERA

A PAULA WISEMAN BOOK
SIMON & SCHUSTER BOOKS FOR YOUNG READERS
NEW YORK LONDON TORONTO SYDNEY NEW DELHI

SIMON & SCHUSTER BOOKS FOR YOUNG READERS
An imprint of Simon & Schuster Children's Publishing Division
1230 Avenue of the Americas, New York, New York 10020
This book is a work of fiction. Any references to historical events,
real people, or real places are used fictitiously. Other names, characters,
places, and events are products of the author's imagination, and any resemblance
to actual events or places or persons, living or dead, is entirely coincidental.
Copyright © 2012 by Elise Primavera
All rights reserved, including the right of reproduction
in whole or in part in any form.
SIMON & SCHUSTER BOOKS FOR YOUNG READERS
is a trademark of Simon & Schuster, Inc.
For information about special discounts for bulk purchases, please contact Simon
& Schuster Special Sales at 1-866-506-1949 or business@simonandschuster.com.
The Simon & Schuster Speakers Bureau can bring authors to your live event. For
more information or to book an event, contact the Simon & Schuster Speakers
Bureau at 1-866-248-3049 or visit our website at www.simonspeakers.com.
Also available in a Simon & Schuster Books for Young Readers hardcover edition
Book design by Krista Vossen
The text for this book is set in Stempek Garamond.
The illustrations for this book are rendered in pen and ink.
Manufactured in the United States of America
0815 OFF
First Simon & Schuster Books for Young Readers
paperback edition September 2015
2 4 6 8 10 9 7 5 3 1
The Library of Congress has cataloged the hardcover edition as follows:
Primavera, Elise.
Libby of High Hopes / Elise Primavera.
p. cm.
"A Paula Wiseman Book."
Summary: When ten-year-old Libby Thump stumbles upon
High Hopes Horse Farm and finds her dream horse, Princess, a prize-winning
jumping horse that has been put out to pasture, Libby tries to
convince her parents to give her riding lessons.
ISBN 978-1-4169-5542-9 (hc)
[1. Horses—Fiction. 2. Horsemanship—Fiction.] I. Title.
II. Title: Libby of High Hopes
PZ7.P9354Li 2012
[Fic]—dc23
2011043908
ISBN 978-1-4169-5544-3 (pbk)
ISBN 978-1-4424-5219-0 (eBook)

For my best riding friends, Martha Bishop,
Andi Gilman, and Jane Sleeper, who were and
always will be full of high hopes.

1

LIBBY MEETS A PRINCESS

Libby Thump wished for horses. She sat on the floor of her bedroom surrounded by pictures of them. Grays, chestnuts, bays, piebalds, cantering, trotting, whinnying, sleeping horses!

Up on their shelves forgotten dolls in glittery tiaras gazed out. From under the bed peeked dress-up clothes that Libby and her ex–best friend, Brittany, used to play princess in. But Libby hadn't played princess in a long time. She had been drawing horses.

"Li-i-ibby-y-y-y-y!" her mother called.

"Coming," she replied.

Libby put down her colored chalks and gave the drawing one last look. The horse galloped under blue skies—a horse so white it almost looked pink. She scratched her nose, then pressed her lips together in disapproval. The horse's legs were all wrong. She'd have to fix that when she got back.

"Li-i-ibby-y-y-y-y! For the twentieth time—take the dog for a wa-a-a-a-a-a-alk!" her mother called again.

Libby pulled on a jacket and caught her reflection in the mirror. She had brown eyes that were almost black, long dark braids to her waist, and a big pink smudge across her nose. She wiped it off with one sleeve. Out in the hall Margaret the dog wagged her tail in anticipation.

"And don't let her off the leash!" Libby's older sister, Laurel, reminded her.

Libby and Margaret headed to the park. As soon

as they entered, she unclipped the leash. *Imagine,* she thought, picking up a stick, *being on a leash your entire life.* Margaret wagged her tail furiously, ready for a chase, and Libby threw the stick. It was a really good throw—in fact, so good that it was one of the reasons Libby's life was about to change forever.

Up, up into the trees the stick rose ever higher, landing far out, past the path, off into the woods, and Margaret went merrily after it. This was a problem too because no one in the family had ever been able to get her to come unless they were holding a slab of roast beef or a carton of ice cream.

Libby cupped her hands around her mouth: "Margaret!" She gingerly picked her way through some brush and came to a narrow dirt trail. "Come on, girl," she called again, hoping that Margaret would actually listen for a change.

Why did I let her off the leash? Libby scolded herself.

She reached the edge of the woods, and thankfully,

there on the other side of a five-railed fence, stick proudly in her mouth, was Margaret. Libby climbed the fence, and now she and the dog were in a large open field—but it didn't take long to see that they were not alone.

A huge horse raised its head and stared at the intruders. Its once-white coat was now caked with dried mud, and its long mane separated into strands as thick as sausages; its yellowed, tangled tail reached almost to the ground. The horse shied and then swung around on its haunches to face them from a few feet back.

Now, Margaret led a fairly sheltered life and she had no idea how much damage a kick from a horse could cause. She let the stick fall from her mouth and ran at the horse with the idea of nipping its ankles, but the horse wheeled again and this time bolted across the field. For a second Margaret was stunned, she couldn't believe that something this big was actually running away from her, and then she did what she always did when something ran away from her—she chased it.

"Margaret! No!" Libby screamed.

The horse was running so fast that Libby could actually feel the vibration of its hooves in her own legs, and it occurred to her that something really bad could very well happen. She had to put a stop to this.

The horse galloped by with Margaret right behind, and Libby lunged for her.

"Gotcha!" She tackled the dog and quickly located the ring for the leash to clip her back onto it.

But the frightened horse kept going. Libby's mouth went dry and she held tightly to Margaret. Like a runaway train, the horse was headed straight for the five-rail, *very* solid fence. If the horse crashed into it and was hurt—or worse—it would be Libby's fault.

"Stop . . . please stop!" she cried.

Three strides . . . two . . . The horse put its legs out in front of it, chipping into the ground, trying to stop. Libby covered her eyes but then couldn't help looking, and gasped because an instant later the animal sprang with amazing agility over the huge fence with room to spare. The horse hovered in the air, front legs tucked tightly under, its tail fanned out behind. It landed soundlessly a great distance past the other side of the fence, galloped down the slope, and thundered out of sight.

Of course Libby ran after the horse—she had to— she had to make sure that someone knew it was loose. What if it got out to the road? What if it got lost?

Down the hill with Margaret in tow Libby raced, her long dark braids whipping in the wind. She wished that she'd never gone on this stupid walk, let Margaret off the stupid leash, or thrown the stupid stick.

Libby wished she were home, sitting on the floor surrounded by her pictures of horses, quietly drawing in her room, with the dolls all around, like princesses in their glittery tiaras.

What Libby Thump didn't know was that there in the field she had just met a princess—one without a tiara.

She also didn't know that her life was about to change forever.

2

LIBBY'S LIFE CHANGES FOREVER

But before Libby's life changed forever, she got into trouble.

She was in trouble with Sal—he was the white horse's owner, and by now it had skidded into the fence of the riding ring. He had seen the whole thing from where he shoveled manure onto a giant pile near the barn.

"Come with me," Sal said. This was after Libby tried to explain about throwing the stick, and Margaret getting lost, and the horse jumping out of the field (she left out the part about letting the dog off the leash).

Sal led Libby and Margaret and the white horse into the barn.

Ordinarily, Libby would have been excited to see the horses in their stalls munching hay, but right now she was too afraid to enjoy the experience. Right now she felt as though she was on her way to the principal's office—a principal who looked like a pirate. With his heavy black boots, dark black hair, and weathered face, all Sal was missing was the bandanna and the earring.

Inside the barn Sal handed the horse, still breathing heavily, to a stocky girl with blond, frizzy hair who looked a little bit older than Libby's sister, Laurel, but younger than her mother.

"Emily, you'd better walk her until she's cool," he said brusquely. "Then turn her back out."

"Sure, Sal," Emily mumbled.

As the horse walked by, it kept Libby in sight with an uneasy look and Libby recalled what she'd once heard about horses being able to sense people's feelings.

"This way," Sal said.

He led Libby into a room that smelled of leather. A row of saddles sat on racks against one wall and heaps of bridles hung from two hooks attached to the ceiling. Large squares of cotton saddle pads stiff with sweat and horsehair were strewn about, along with brushes and other paraphernalia that Libby couldn't put a name to. She thought the place could use a good cleaning.

"Sit," Sal ordered.

Margaret sat and so did Libby, marveling, for she hadn't ever realized the dog knew the meaning of the word.

"In the first place, the horse did *not* jump over any fence," he said.

"But he *did*!" Libby insisted.

"She," corrected Sal. "Her name is Princess."

Libby wanted to say that "Princess" must be having a bad hair day, but she dared not. Libby reasoned, "If she didn't jump over the fence, how did she get out of the field?"

"There's a gate at the bottom of the field that she uses to get to her shed—and in the second place," Sal continued, "you are always supposed to have your dog on a leash."

Libby nervously switched Margaret's leash into her other hand to look like she was doing a really good job of holding on to it now. Feeling uncomfortable, Libby averted her eyes. The walls were covered with blue ribbons of all different lengths, but thick cobwebs obscured the writing of each horse show they had been won at. Dusty framed photos of horses jumping huge fences hung haphazardly about the room. Suddenly Libby noticed that all the horses in the photos were Princess!

"But isn't that her jumping?" Libby asked.

"Princess was a champion show jumper. These are all her ribbons. But there was an accident," Sal said flatly. "She had a bad fall . . . and now she's just old . . . she's washed up."

"But I saw her—she jumped, she really did!" Libby said earnestly.

"If she did, it'd pretty much be a miracle—keep your dog on a leash from now on."

Sal got up, signaling the end to the conversation, and this is the part where Libby's life changed forever, because without even thinking she blurted out, "Do you give pony rides?"

"I used to give riding lessons." Sal left the room.

"But you don't anymore?" Libby called, and tried to catch up to him.

"No." Sal walked down the aisle of the barn and Libby noticed for the first time that he had a bad limp.

Libby and Margaret walked behind. "But why not?"

"Because it was a long time ago." Sal picked up some hay and started to throw a section at a time into each stall.

Libby knew how it was if she didn't draw for a while—it was as if she had forgotten. She didn't want to hurt Sal's feelings, but she had to ask, "Did you forget how to ride?"

"Yes, I forgot how to ride." Sal took the hose that was curled up in the corner. He put it through the bars of a stall. Libby and Margaret watched attentively as he filled the water bucket.

"But you're wearing riding pants and riding boots—it sure looks like you've been riding, doesn't it, Margaret?" Margaret wagged her tail and Libby decided Sal was teasing her. "You didn't forget how to ride," she said like she'd just gotten the joke.

Sal said nothing. The water bucket was full, so he went to the next stall.

Libby and Margaret went with him. "So then why don't you give lessons anymore, huh?"

"Because I *don't*," Sal said, exasperated. "Now go along home, little girl."

"I'm ten years old—almost eleven!" Libby wanted to make the point that she was *not* a little girl. She stuck out her hand to shake. "My name's Libby."

Sal ignored the extended hand. "Go *home*, Libby!" *He said that a little too meanly,* Libby thought.

14

Libby bit the side of her lip. She turned to go and then got an idea. "What if I come back with my parents?"

There was silence.

"My parents will tell you how I love horses and draw them all the time and I'm the best in my class and everything. . . ."

"Suit yourself." Sal shrugged. He pointed with his thumb over his shoulder. "The way out is down the driveway."

"Yay!" Libby cheered. "Thanks, Sal—thanks! I'll see you soon!"

Once outside Libby and Margaret set off down the rutted dirt driveway. Libby saw the girl let Princess back into the field. The horse went to stand under an old sagging shed in a muddy paddock. Libby *knew* she had seen the horse jump that big post-and-rail fence in the field. Maybe Princess was better from her injury—Sal just didn't know it. Maybe she could be a champion show jumper again!

Suddenly Libby's future spread out before her in sparkling clarity. She could imagine just how it would happen, too. She would start by taking lessons and Sal would be astonished by her extraordinary natural ability. She would convince Sal that Princess was all better and he would insist that Libby start riding her in horse shows.

Libby could just see herself on Princess going over those enormous jumps like in the photos. She could hear her name being announced over the loud speaker, "And first place goes to Libby Thump, riding Princess!"

Libby and Margaret had reached the end of the driveway. Hanging from a crooked post in a patch of weeds was a sign with the name of the farm on it.

"High Hopes Horse Farm," Libby whispered.

She tugged impatiently at Margaret. She had to hurry home to ask her parents to let her take riding lessons.

3

RIDING LESSONS???

W hatever happened to the piano lessons that you couldn't live without?" her mother asked. The family had finished eating dinner and Libby's mother darted around the kitchen putting things away. She worked as a personal trainer at the local gym and was still in her workout clothes, her hair yanked up into a ponytail. "Now we have a piano that no one wants to play."

"Yes, but I was awful at piano," Libby reminded her.

"You were awful because you didn't concentrate enough on it," Libby's father said.

"I agree," said Libby's mother. "By now you could be playing as well as Brittany—maybe even better—if you would just apply yourself."

Libby frowned. She didn't like being compared with her ex–best friend, Brittany, just because *her* mom and *Brittany's* mom were *best* friends.

Mrs. Thump busied herself clearing the table.

Libby hopped onto the kitchen counter and swung her legs. This was going to be a lot harder than she thought it was going to be. "But, Mom, this is different—you know how much I love horses."

Mrs. Thump's face softened. She did know how much Libby loved horses. When her younger daughter wasn't drawing horses, she was galloping around the backyard like one. But it was hard to get Libby to listen sometimes. "Honey, how many times have I told you not to sit on the counter?"

"You're right, Mom." Libby hopped off and rolled

up her sleeves. It was time to try a new tactic. She started to load the dishes into the dishwasher, being her most helpful, agreeable self.

"You might want to wash the car when you're done there, Lib." Her father winked at her.

"I can wash the car!" Libby offered.

"I'm kidding." Her father playfully pulled one braid before going out to his office, a converted toolshed in the backyard. He had a landscaping business, but lately he spent more time trying to drum up customers.

Libby picked up the sponge and wiped off the table. "So, Mom?"

A smile flickered across her mother's face. "How much does it cost for riding lessons?"

"Riding lessons?" Laurel stood in the doorway to the kitchen sending a text on her phone. She finally looked up. "Did someone say 'riding lessons'?"

"I want to take riding lessons over at High Hopes Horse Farm—I'm trying to talk Mom and Dad into going over there with me." Libby put her hands together as if in prayer and gave her mom her most angelic smile.

"I want to go," Laurel said.

"You *do*?" said Libby and her mother at the same time. They were both flabbergasted—Laurel was fourteen and never wanted to do anything besides text her friends and stare at herself in the mirror.

"Yeah, why not?" Laurel ran her fingers through her long blond hair as if she were putting it into a ponytail, only to let it loose again—a habit that Libby found annoying. "It sounds like fun."

"I guess it wouldn't hurt to go look," Mrs. Thump declared. She was happy that Laurel was showing some interest in something besides boys and clothes and hairdos. She felt her forehead and laughed, "Sure you're not coming down with something?"

Laurel was sure.

"YAY!" Libby clapped. Her parents hadn't said yes, but they hadn't said no, either.

They would go this weekend. Now all Libby needed to do was to get through one more day. One more day of school . . . one more day till summer vacation—she knew it was going to feel like a million years.

4
PRINCESS LIBBY

The last day of school—it always felt like it would never get here. But the last day of Mrs. Williams's fourth grade felt like it took a million years.

Libby doodled in her notebook.

"I expect each of you to keep up with your studies, blah, blah, blah. . . ." The "blah, blah, blah" part was pretty much all Libby heard of what Mrs. Williams was saying. She was thinking about High Hopes Horse Farm.

Libby and her best friend, Mim, rolled their eyes at each other and sighed. Mrs. Williams was the only fourth-grade teacher who was actually teaching anything—all the other classes were playing games and doing fun stuff like washing the desks and clearing off the bulletin boards.

"I would recommend that you read at least blah, blah, blah . . ."

Libby looked longingly out the window. Beyond the playground, dew sparkled on the new grass in

the soccer fields. Libby could just see herself riding Princess over those fields faster and faster until it felt like they were flying.

She turned to a clean page in her notebook and started to draw herself and Princess galloping across a field. She was the best in the class at drawing horses and had a whole notebook full of them to prove it.

"And how many books have I recommended?" Mrs. Williams glared at Libby.

Libby had the horse drawn except for its legs — they

were always the hardest to get right. *Let's see, the knees would be bent and her hooves would be off the ground and—*

"Libby?"

Libby suddenly realized that everybody was looking at her. She quickly covered the drawing with her hand. "Um, what was the question?"

Meanwhile, from the other side of the room, someone did know the question *and* the answer.

"Brittany?"

"We should read two books a week, Mrs. Williams."

"Very good, Brittany." Mrs. Williams frowned at Libby.

Libby closed her notebook and tried to appear as though she was paying attention. But she wasn't.

Have you ever had a friend that was better than you at everything? This was how Libby felt about Brittany. Even when they were little kids going to birthday parties together, Libby knew way before the games started who would pin the tail on the donkey and who would be the last one seated in musical chairs. Everybody else knew it too and wanted to be friends with Brittany, until Brittany had ten friends and Libby had one—that would be Brittany. As she got older, Libby got Bs, and Brittany got As. At the beach club Brittany got to win medals in swimming, and Libby got ear infections.

Libby wondered how Brittany could be so good at everything. In fact, drawing horses was probably the only thing that Libby did better than her.

"Libby," Mim whispered when Mrs. Williams turned to walk to the blackboard. She leaned over and handed Libby a note. It said: Did you hear about Brittany's Princess Spa Party—you invited?????

Libby shook her head no. By lunchtime Libby was sure she would be the only girl in the entire class who didn't get invited to the Princess Spa Party—whatever that was.

Finally the day was over. Mrs. Williams handed out report cards and the bell rang.

Libby opened her report card and hoped for once

that she had gotten something besides all Bs, but it was just the same as always. Brittany would have gotten all As, which meant that Brittany's mother would brag to Libby's mother, and then Libby's mother would want to know why Libby didn't get all As. Libby threw the troublesome report card into the bottom of her backpack in frustration and looked for Mim; there was something that Libby wanted to know.

"She's been handing out invites all day." Mim held up a pink envelope and nodded to where Brittany handed out another as if on cue.

"What's a Princess Spa Party, anyway?" she said to Mim in a low voice so no one could hear.

Today was ballet for Mim and she didn't want to be late. She spoke quickly. "They serve pink cupcakes and do your nails and hair—and you're supposed to dress up like a princess."

Libby had never had her nails or hair done and couldn't help feeling like it would be really fun, but the other part . . .

"Dress up like a princess?!" Libby made a funny face and Mim made one back.

Mim hoisted her backpack over her shoulder and turned to leave, then remembered, "Did you get a teacher's comment on your report card?"

Libby hadn't.

"Mrs. Williams said she enjoyed having me in her class this year!" Mim said proudly.

"That's great!" Libby tried to sound happy for Mim, but she was a little worried. *Teacher's comment?* She hadn't seen *that* on *her* report card, maybe she'd better look again! She was just about to do this when someone touched her shoulder.

"Hey, Libby." Brittany held a pink envelope. "This is for you."

Two girls yelled, "Brit!" They were running down the hall outside to the buses. "Come on!" they shouted impatiently.

Before Libby could say anything, Brittany ran off.

The envelope was addressed in gold curlicue letters to

"Princess Libby." Pink and silver glitter sprinkled out when she opened it. The card popped up into a fairy-tale castle with a princess wearing a pink veil made of real material that looked like a ballerina's tutu. It was the most beautiful invitation that Libby had ever seen! It said:

Her Royal Highness, Princess Brittany, invites you to her castle to celebrate the 11th anniversary of her birth!

When: Sunday, July 29th

Where: HRH's castle

For a Princess Spa Party!

Wear your finest princess attire.

Suddenly Libby was aware that her hands were slightly sweaty. She wiped her moist palms on her pants. Flecks of glitter came off her fingers and stuck to the denim.

Libby couldn't help feeling relieved that she'd gotten the invite, and she couldn't help liking the idea of getting her nails and hair done—eating pink cupcakes didn't sound too bad either.

There was only one thing.

She brushed the glitter off her jeans and left the room. Libby was sure there was only *one* reason she had been invited and that was because her mom and Brittany's mom were best friends.

Once Libby realized that, she didn't want to go to the party at all. But there would be no getting out of it—her mom would have a fit if she didn't go. And . . . what do you wear to a Princess Spa Party, anyway?

Libby got on the bus and sat all the way in the back, where she wouldn't have to speak to anybody. Then she remembered her report card and thought, *Maybe*

Mrs. Williams said she enjoyed having me in her class too! Libby fished the report card out of her backpack and with hope in her heart read the following:

> I have enjoyed having Libby in my
> class this year.
> But Libby needs to apply
> herself. Sometimes she does not
> pay attention or follow directions
> as well as she should.
> Libby needs to live up to her
> potential!

Potential? What was that? Libby looked the word up as soon as she got home.

po·ten·tial pə-ˈten(t)-shəl
adj. 1. expressing possibility; *specifically*: of, relating to, or constituting a verb phrase expressing possibility
n. 1. something that can develop or become actual

Libby closed the dictionary. *Hmmmm, something that can develop,* Libby thought, *expressing possibility— what kind of possibilities?* Libby thought about it some more. At least on the one hand she *had* potential, on the other hand not living up to it, not paying attention, and not following directions weren't so hot. And how was she supposed to "live up" to her potential if she didn't even know what her potential was?

Her mother was not home from the gym yet, which was actually lucky for two reasons. One, she wouldn't have to show her the report card yet, and two, she wouldn't have to take suggestions from her on what to wear to Brittany's party.

Besides, Libby didn't want to dress up like a princess— what were they in, first grade? She collapsed on her bed and groaned.

There was only one thing to do. Libby put the invitation out of her mind. She would think about it later. She had made it through the day, and tomorrow they were going to High Hopes Horse Farm!

5

HIGH HOPES

In the morning Libby sat in the car with Margaret and her family as they traveled down the uneven dirt driveway to the farm. The car shook and rattled, hitting one deep pothole after another.

"It looks sort of like a dump." Laurel scrunched up her nose and stuck out her tongue.

"Look!" Libby pointed. "There's Princess!"

Margaret sat at attention next to Libby and held her head up so she could see out the window at the horse grazing in the field. Margaret made a low growl.

"I'll bet Margaret would love to get loose and go chase that horse," Mr. Thump commented. "We should probably keep her in the car."

"Yeah, probably." Libby laughed nervously and was glad that when they stopped a moment later, the topic was dropped.

They parked next to an ancient-looking tractor. Now even Libby could see that the farm was run down. Rails were missing in the fence of the riding ring. Weeds grew in patches alongside the entire length of the barn. An old horse trailer sat rusting in a corner under a dead tree. The place looked forlorn and deserted.

"Can I help you?" Sal limped out of the barn pushing a wheelbarrow full of manure.

"I told you I'd bring my parents, so here they are!" Libby exclaimed.

Sal walked the wheelbarrow over to the enormous manure pile and pushed it on its nose to empty the

contents. He started back to barn, and as he passed Libby and her family, he mumbled, "Sal Ricci, nice to meet you."

"We were wondering about riding lessons?" Mr. Thump said.

Sal just kept walking and disappeared into the barn.

"Let's go," Laurel whispered to her mother.

"Wait," Libby pleaded.

"Libby!" Mrs. Thump shouted.

It was too late. Libby had already run after Sal.

Inside, the barn was cool and dim. Cobwebs hung from the joists of a hayloft and mice skittered along the beams overhead. The short, stocky girl, whom Sal had called Emily the other day, was brushing a horse in the aisle. She looked up and smiled when she saw it was Libby with her family. Sal completely ignored them.

Mr. and Mrs. Thump and Laurel stood in the barn looking around as if they had just landed on another planet.

Margaret started to bark in the car, and Mr. Thump

glanced in that direction. "We should go, Mr. Ricci is busy."

"He's not busy!" Libby watched Sal park the wheelbarrow outside an empty stall.

"We're sorry to barge in on you like this," Mrs. Thump said, and frowned at Libby.

Sal threw clumps of manure into the wheelbarrow with a pitchfork. "You have a very persistent daughter," he said.

"We know," Mr. and Mrs. Thump replied at the same time.

Sal threw out a load of the soiled shavings with one big heave. "*Very* persistent."

"And that's good, right?" Libby wanted Sal to like her. She thought that being "very persistent" was always a good thing—but something in the way he had said it made her not so sure. Sal put down the pitchfork, and for the first time he looked Libby straight in the eye. It was as if all those years around horses had given him a sort of sixth sense about people. Libby looked him straight in the eye back without even blinking.

"Huh," Sal said, breaking the stare. "Guess I'm not busy—haven't been busy for three years."

Emily looked up, surprised, from where she had been brushing off the horse.

Sal stood with his hands on his hips and studied Libby. "You want to learn how to ride a horse?"

"Yes! More than anything in the world!" Libby said earnestly.

"Me too!" Laurel added. She had been standing with her parents and now came up behind Libby.

Libby held her breath. Her parents just had to say yes to the riding lessons.

Libby's parents did say yes—just not to her.

"Can I take lessons?" Laurel asked her parents excitedly.

Her mother and father looked at each other.

"Y-Yes, if you really want to," her mother stammered.

"What about me?" The horror of what was happening started to dawn on Libby.

"Libby, you're only ten years old, you have plenty of time to have lessons if you really want them," Mrs. Thump said calmly.

"Your mother's right," said her father. "Laurel is older and we can't afford lessons for you both right now."

"But it was my idea!" Libby's eyes filled with tears. "It's not fair!"

"Now, Libby . . . ," Mr. Thump started to say, "that's enough," and he had an expression on his face that said he meant business.

But then Sal stepped in and said, "I've got an idea."

6

SAL'S IDEA

What do you think about when you are riding a pony for forty-five minutes and only allowed to walk in a circle while your sister takes a lesson? If you are Libby Thump, you think that someday you are going to be the Best Rider in the Entire World. And you think about the look on Brittany's face when she sees you on TV winning your gold medal at the Olympics.

By now you've probably figured out Sal's idea:

Libby was allowed to ride a pony for free during Laurel's lesson. While Laurel got to take riding lessons on the beautiful chestnut horse named Summer, Libby was left to walk in dusty circles riding a scruffy, fat pony named Cough Drop.

No. It was not fair.

Cough Drop didn't seem too happy about the arrangement either. He and Libby were soon in a battle to stay away from the gate and go to where Cough Drop wanted to go—back to his stall in the barn.

But Sal wasn't the only one with an idea. Libby had an idea too. She watched Laurel, and if Sal told Laurel to keep her elbows in, then Libby kept her elbows in. If he told Laurel to move her left leg back, then Libby did that too. Whatever Sal told Laurel to do Libby did, because Libby's idea was to pretend that Sal was giving *her* a lesson.

By the end of Laurel's lesson Libby had learned how to hold the reins, to keep her heels down, to keep her legs back, and to look up. From Cough Drop she learned how to keep him from pulling her forward to reach down and eat grass.

Sal had Laurel and Libby come into the center of the ring just as a woman on a shiny bay horse appeared. For a moment Libby hardly even recognized the rider. Gone was the short, stocky girl. Dressed in her tan breeches and tall black boots, the frizzy hair tucked up inside her black velvet riding helmet, Emily had been transformed!

"Is that Emily's horse?" Libby asked Sal.

"Yes, that's Benson—he was her show horse," Sal answered.

"Does Emily still show him?" Libby asked.

"No," Sal replied. There was an edge to his voice and Laurel gave Libby a look.

"But he's *so* beautiful—" Libby continued.

"Libby, hush up!" Laurel said through clenched teeth.

I can't even say anything, Libby thought, but she kept it to herself.

"Just watch!" Laurel hissed.

Emily trotted over some fences while Sal set up a huge gate with a rail over it. Before long Emily was jumping a course of fences. She cantered a half circle and jumped over the gate with ease. Libby tried to see how Emily got Benson to turn and loop around and meet each fence at just the right stride. Emily was such a quiet rider there were absolutely no outward signals or other signs you could see her giving the horse. The only evidence was Benson's ears, which flicked back and forth as he was given commands. Libby thought it was as if Emily and Benson had a secret language—just like she and Mim when they exchanged notes in Mrs. Williams's class!

Libby watched Sal watch Emily, and she could see the admiration in his face. She decided that Emily was probably the Best Rider in the Entire World. Right then and there Libby made up her mind that she wanted to be just like Emily.

Libby tried to sit on Cough Drop just like Emily sat

on Benson. She put her shoulders back and her chin up, just like Emily. She pushed her heels down and kept her elbows in, just like Emily. On the way back to the barn Libby glanced at Sal to see if he'd noticed how perfect her position was now, just like Emily's.

But Sal didn't notice.

So Libby got another idea.

By Laurel's second lesson Libby knew that if she was going to be the Best Rider in the Entire World, just like Emily, she would need to know how to trot.

"Hey, Sal, can I try to trot?" Libby asked.

"Not now." Sal was removing Laurel's stirrups—today she was going to ride without them to make her legs stronger.

"Can I trot later?"

"Maybe."

"Like when?"

Silence.

"Can I trot later?" Libby waited for an answer.

But there was no answer. Laurel didn't even yell at

her like she usually did. Nobody noticed Libby no matter what she did!

Which brought Libby to the next conclusion: Since Sal never noticed anything that she did, he probably wouldn't notice that she was trotting, either.

Libby decided she would try an experiment! She squeezed her legs like she'd heard Sal tell Laurel a bunch of times. Cough Drop put his ears back but did walk a little faster, and a little faster until he started to trot. Libby bounced and bounced and bounced until she felt like a milk shake! Up, down, up, down—she'd seen Laurel practice posting at the walk, and then she'd been able to post at the trot easy-peasy, but it was a whole lot harder than it looked. Laurel had picked it up right away—she wasn't bouncing all over the place. In fact, Laurel was doing really well! Libby pulled the reins but Cough Drop didn't stop. He'd had enough—he was going to the gate and back to the barn to his stall whether Libby liked it or not! He went right past Sal, and Libby held her breath.

But Sal said nothing—he was watching Laurel instead. "Very good!" he praised her. Laurel had gone around the ring posting—without stirrups!

It was as plain as the nose on Libby's face; her sister, Laurel, had Potential! Laurel had Potential to be the Best Rider in the Entire World, just like Emily, and Libby did not.

Emily gave Cough Drop a bath, and Libby sat on

the old mounting block with her chin in her hands.

"How'd Cough Drop go today?" Emily asked.

"Okay," Libby muttered.

"Just okay?" Emily dunked her sponge in a bucket of soapy water. Suds dripped off the sponge.

"Yeah," Libby answered.

Emily soaped up Cough Drop's back. "When I was your age, I rode a pony like Cough Drop and he ran away with me straight back to the barn every single day."

"Really?" Libby couldn't believe that a rider as good as Emily had had the same thing happen to her. "You mean you weren't good at it right away?"

"Heavens no!" Emily laughed. "I was awful in the beginning, but I loved it anyway. Gosh, I practically lived at the barn when I was your age."

"You did?" Libby perked up her ears.

"Yep. I hung around, did stalls, groomed horses." Emily got the hose and rinsed the pony off. "That's how I learned about horses!"

"Will you teach me everything you know, Emily?" Libby said eagerly.

"How about you start with stall cleaning?" Sal said. He had overheard them while he was hosing off Summer.

"Yuck!" Laurel cried.

"Great idea!" Libby added quickly. She was thrilled even to clean a stall—but just then her mother pulled up in the car. It was time to go.

"Can't I stay?" Libby begged. "Sal just had a great idea!"

But Libby's mother did not think Sal's idea was great—at all. She ordered them to the car and headed home.

Libby sat in the backseat like a dark thundercloud. Emily had said she practically lived at the barn when she was Libby's age. Emily would've been at the barn right now learning stuff, Libby thought—learning Everything There Was to Know About Horses, and now Emily was the Best Rider in the Entire World!

Wait a minute . . . yes—that was it! Libby sat up and laughed. Laurel turned around and looked at her like she was crazy.

But Libby wasn't crazy, she had figured out something—something really, *really* important—and now Libby Thump would let nothing stand in her way!

At home Libby could hardly eat her lunch she was so excited.

"You can come with me to the gym," her mother said.

"You can come with me to the beach," Laurel said.

"I think I'll go over to Mim's house," Libby said casually.

But Libby did not go over to her best friend Mim's house. As soon as Libby's mother left for the gym, and

Laurel left for the beach, Libby took off for the park, through the woods, under the rail fence, and across the field—back to the barn.

"Hi, Princess!" she called, and the white horse looked up when she passed.

But when Libby reached the barn, all her excitement vanished and she felt a little scared. She knew she would be in big trouble if her mom found out where she was. But how would she ever get to be the Best Rider in the Entire World, just like Emily, riding around in circles on Cough Drop just one day a week? Great riders needed to be brave and she would start right now!

Libby looked inside the doorway to the barn, but no one was around. She walked down the aisle and read the name tags on the stall doors of all the horses. There was Benson, Cough Drop, Summer, and some other horses she didn't know yet. Libby closed her eyes and took a deep breath through her nose. She couldn't imagine a better smell—the smell of horses, and hay, and shavings, and oats. Libby sighed. She wished that she knew how to clean a stall and how to put a saddle on, how to canter—everything! Libby rubbed her arms; it was a hot day but she had goose bumps. She couldn't explain it, but she had the strongest feeling that something really wonderful could happen to her here at High Hopes Horse Farm—she knew that this was a place where she could Live Up to Her Potential!

Suddenly there was a sharp sound. She thought it might be Sal or Emily, but it wasn't. There at the end of the barn a man was standing by a stall. At once all her courage vanished and she felt the urge to hide. She slid down next to a trunk and watched.

The man pushed the bolt on the door and led the horse out of the stall. *Clip, clop! Clip, clop!* Coming right toward Libby was the most gigantic horse she had ever seen in her life. He was a deep brown color with a black mane and tail. His head reached up almost as high as the hayloft and was twice the size of Cough Drop's.

As they walked, the man talked to him like he was a person. "How's your day going, George?" The horse swished his tail in response. The man walked slowly, if not a little unsteadily, and there was no mistaking the bowed legs underneath his perfectly pressed jeans.

The horse loomed over Libby now and she could see his feet were as big as platters, with large, bony growths on the insides of his legs. He had a deep sway in his back and his hip bones stuck out.

The man's hair was all white and he looked very old. He had tanned, leathery skin that reminded Libby of a walnut.

The man took a carrot out of his pocket and held it for the horse. The horse wriggled his giant lips and Libby could see his big, square yellow teeth. The carrot vanished and the old man produced another.

"What do you say we clean you up?" Ropes hung on either side of the aisle, and the man snapped them to the animal's halter. Then he turned toward Libby, who was still crouching by the trunk. "What have we here?" he said, surprised.

"I'm Libby and I take lessons—I mean my sister

does—Sal lets me ride Cough Drop and all. . . ." Libby fumbled her words.

"Does he?" The man helped her up. "I'm Mr. McClave, and I'll bet you're a good little jockey." He chuckled. "But you're sitting on my grooming kit!"

"He sure is a big horse." Libby dusted off her pants.

"This is General George—say hello, George." The horse bobbed his head up and down, and the man gave him another carrot.

"Wow!" Libby was impressed. "He must be really fun to ride!"

"Oh, I don't ride him—I just come to visit and groom the old boy. I haven't ridden him since he was twenty-five."

"How old is he?" Libby asked.

"He's twenty-eight if he's a day!" Mr. McClave held the back of his hand to the side of his mouth and whispered, "That's very old for a horse, but don't tell him."

"I won't," Libby whispered back.

Mr. McClave broke a carrot and gave Libby a piece.

"Hold your hand flat so he doesn't mistake one of those fingers for a carrot."

Libby held her hand out flat, and he wriggled his lips just like before and the carrot was gone in an instant.

"Don't you ever get bored just grooming him?" Libby wanted to know.

"Not at all. I don't just groom him, I talk to him too."

"Talk to a horse?" Libby had never heard of that before.

"I'll tell you a little secret." Mr. McClave took a round, rubbery-looking tool with rows of teeth and started to rub the horse's coat in circles. "Sometimes talking to a horse is a whole lot better than talking to another person because horses listen—and they know how you feel."

"What do you say to George?" Libby asked.

"All kinds of things, but mostly I talk about the good old days."

"What are the good old days?"

Mr. McClave took out another brush and with a sweeping motion started brushing all the dirt and loose hair off the horse. He talked as he worked.

"George and I go back a long time. I bought him when he was a four-year-old. You should have seen him back then—full of vim and vigor. I guess we both were."

Libby sat on a bale of hay and watched. "Did you go to horse shows and win a lot of ribbons?"

"Nah, we used to foxhunt—I was master of fox-hounds around here."

"Fox? I've never even seen a fox!" Libby exclaimed.

"Me neither," Mr. McClave chuckled. "We never caught one, but we had a marvelous time galloping around for miles in every kind of weather!"

"Is George a good jumper?"

"He could jump any ditch or five-rail fence that we came across out there."

The longer Mr. McClave worked on the big horse, the lower General George's head hung, and his eyes began to look sleepy.

"I think he likes that!" Libby stroked his nose and it felt like velvet. There were deep hollows above the old horse's eyes, and the hair had turned white.

Libby watched while Mr. McClave picked up each of General George's huge feet, using a metal tool with a hooked end, called a hoof-pick, to clean out all the dirt in his hooves. He took a paintbrush out of a can of dark, smelly liquid and painted each hoof. "This is hoof dressing. It's good for their feet."

"It looks like he has on patent-leather shoes," Libby said.

General George was wide awake now and stood proudly—it was as if he knew he was all spiffed up and handsome again. "Done!" Mr. McClave said. "You know, I'd love to be close to my kids, who live three states away, but I could never move George—he's too old to be uprooted."

"Couldn't you just leave him here and come to visit?" Libby asked.

"Leave George? Never! He's the only one who remembers the good old days!" The horse nuzzled Mr. McClave. "There now," he said softly, and patted George's neck.

Libby had an idea. "Do you have any pictures of General George from the good old days?"

Mr. McClave cleaned off the brushes he had just used and put them all back in his kit. "You really want to see pictures, do you?"

"I like to draw horses. . . ." Libby felt a little shy asking, but she'd gone this far. "So maybe I could draw General George—if you don't mind or anything?"

"Mind? I think it would be terrific! I've had some of the happiest moments of my life riding this horse." Mr. McClave looked at George affectionately. "He could go all day . . . but now . . . neither one of us can do that—we're both long in the tooth."

"What's long in the tooth?" Libby asked.

"Old!" Mr. McClave ruffled Libby's hair.

He gave Libby some carrots to feed the other horses just as Emily came walking up the aisle carrying a few sections of hay. "What are you doing back here?"

Libby held up the carrots and replied, "I'm here to give these carrots to Princess."

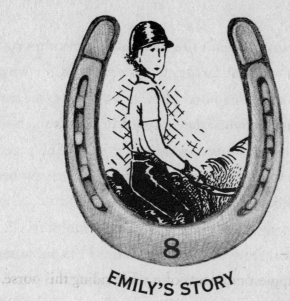

8
EMILY'S STORY

Emily was on her way out to feed Princess and she let Libby tag along. Libby rattled off all the brushes and grooming tools that she had just learned about. "Currycomb, dandy brush, body brush, mane comb, water brush, hoof-pick, and a rub rag to make them shine—oh, and hoof dressing."

They walked out behind the barn, where Libby had never been till now. Old farm equipment lay in various states of disrepair. Weeds grew up through the center of an old tractor tire, and poles from jumps rotted under vines. It looked like a graveyard for what was once a thriving horse farm. It was a sad place and Libby was glad when they reached Princess's shed.

The white mare was waiting for them. She paced back and forth in front of the gate. Emily threw her the hay and went to check her water.

"How long have you worked here?" Libby asked.

"About three years." Emily dumped the old water from the horse's two buckets. She rinsed them out at the pump and began filling them.

Libby stood on the bottom rail of the fence and hung her arms over the top rail as she watched Emily. "Were you here when Princess had her fall?"

Emily took a deep breath and then exhaled slowly. "I was at the show that day."

"What happened?" Libby asked softly.

Emily hooked the buckets one at a time back onto the fence. "It was bad. Sal was riding Princess at a really big show. She had been winning all over the

place—everybody wanted to buy her. Sal even got offered two hundred thousand dollars for her, but he would never sell—he loved that horse."

Emily leaned against the fence and recalled the day. "Sal had tons of students back then too. It wasn't at all like it is now." She squinted into the late-afternoon sun as if she were watching the scene play out all over again. "Sal was riding Princess in a jumper class, the fences were huge. It had rained the night before. The ground was slick. He was in a timed jump-off with one other rider for first place. Sal pushed her hard, but Princess could handle it—until they got to this one difficult fence. He had to make a sharp turn to get to it. They went around the corner and her back feet slipped; he tried to hold her together, but there were only two strides to get it right. Princess suddenly put in another stride at the spot where she was supposed to take off." Emily was quiet for a moment and all Libby could hear was the steady crunch of Princess eating her hay. "She caught a bunch of rails and went down. She fell on Sal and he was hurt really badly."

"But if she was such a great jumper, why did she fall?" Libby asked.

"It was an accident," Emily said sadly. "Sal blamed himself for pushing her. . . ."

"What happened to Sal?"

"He had a vertebra in his back broken and his leg in three places." Emily pointed to where. "He's got pins and metal holding that leg together. He's lucky he can walk."

"What about Princess?"

"She wasn't hurt that badly, but like I said, Sal was laid up for a long, long time—he lost everything, his students, his boarders. Mr. McClave is his last. Then Princess foundered badly."

"What's foundered?" Libby had never heard of that before.

"It's a really awful thing that happens to a horse's front hooves if it's left in the stall too long and fed too much—if Sal had been here to look after her, it never would have happened. Once a horse founders, its showing career is finished."

"Poor Princess," Libby said. "Sal must have felt awful!"

"He did."

Princess came over as if she knew they were talking about her. Libby broke off a piece of carrot and offered it just the way Mr. McClave had shown her.

"How did you meet Sal?" Libby asked.

"Sal and I used to compete against each other on the show circuit. We both thought we were going to be the greatest riders in the world!"

"Me too!" Libby said excitedly.

"As you can see, it didn't really work out that way." Emily made a face.

"But you *are* a great rider, Emily!" Libby was sure. She couldn't stop thinking about those high fences that Emily had ridden Benson over the other day.

Emily shook her head. "I was working on a farm giving lessons and whatnot. All the money I had I spent on my horse, Benson—I wanted to compete and still thought I had a shot at getting on the equestrian team, but when I heard about what happened to Princess, I had to help out. That's when I came here, and six months later Sal and I got married."

"You and Sal are *married*?" Libby thought Emily looked so young!

"I'm about thirteen years younger than Sal—he's really aged since the accident. . . ." Emily's voice trailed off as if she was remembering how Sal used to be.

"But Sal is all better now—and so is Princess. I saw her jump that fence up there!" Libby pointed to the post-and-rail up on top of the hill.

"You did?" Emily said with disbelief.

"I really did!" Libby answered. "Sal doesn't believe me, though." Libby told Emily about how Margaret had chased Princess that first day.

"Princess could never compete again, Libby—her feet were too damaged," Emily explained. "But you're right, she is better."

"And so is Sal!" Libby insisted. "Why don't you start to train again?"

"Because Sal doesn't want to." Emily bit the corner of her thumb and looked worried.

"Have you asked him?"

"Have you noticed this place is a mess? We barely have time to take care of the horses, let alone start training seriously for shows." Emily looked defeated.

"But you *can't* give up." Libby knew she was right about this, and Princess raised her head as if she was listening. "Emily—you have to live up to your potential!"

"My what?" Emily laughed.

"Your *potential*!" Libby jumped off the fence. "I'm trying to live up to mine, too!"

Libby held out another piece of carrot to the mare. She patted her neck and flakes of mud crumbled off. "Like Princess—she has the potential to be beautiful again, like she is in the pictures in the tack room." Princess sniffed Libby's pockets for more treats and Libby suddenly got an idea. "Can I make Princess beautiful again?"

Emily came over and handled the mare's long fore-lock, which was stiff with dried mud. "You want to clean up Princess?"

"Yes! More than anything in the world—can I?" Libby was fairly bursting at the seams.

"Well . . ." Emily hesitated.

"Will you help me, Emily, please?"

"Oh, why not." Emily gave in. "The next time you come we'll start—how's that?"

"I can't wait!" Libby squealed. "We'll have a Princess spa party!"

"I guess even a Princess needs to live up to her potential." Emily clapped the mud off her hands.

Just then a car drove up and beeped angrily.

Mrs. Thump got out of the car and shouted across the field, "Libby, I've been looking for you all over the place!"

"Uh-oh," Emily warned. "I think there might be potential for you to be in big trouble."

9

LIBBY GETS IN BIG TROUBLE

Everybody knows that getting into Big Trouble is just another way of saying "You're grounded!" And getting grounded, for Libby Thump, meant not being allowed to go to High Hopes Horse Farm the following week for Laurel's lesson.

Libby's plan to be the Best Rider in the Entire World, just like Emily, was now on hold. So was making Princess beautiful again. Living Up to Her Potential had just gotten her grounded.

No. It was not fair.

On riding lesson day Laurel had already left when Libby was still in her pajamas eating Cheerios and telling Margaret how horribly unfair it all was. Libby heard the screen door slam, and a moment later her mother appeared in the kitchen. She kicked off her sneakers and flopped into a chair with her sports drink.

"How was your run, Mom?" Libby asked. A few mornings a week Libby's mother ran with Brittany's mother, Suzanne.

"Great!" Mrs. Thump said. "But Suzanne is very concerned about Brittany."

Concerned? About Brittany—what else is new? Libby thought.

Mrs. Thump continued, "Brittany's joined the swim team again this year, and it's been *very* hard on her."

"Hard on her?" Libby was all ears. "Why?"

"She really misses you, Libby," Mrs. Thump said.

"Me?" If Libby's mother had just told her that Brittany was growing a second head, she wouldn't have

71

been more surprised. "Wait, let me get this straight—*Brittany* misses *me*?" Libby pointed to herself.

"Yes, honey, she misses you. The other girls are friends but not best friends like when you were little girls."

Libby sat back in her chair trying to absorb what her mother had just said. "So you're saying that Brittany is having a hard time at swim practice because I'm not there."

"Suzanne says Brittany needs a friend." Mrs. Thump finished her drink and got up from the table. "I guess there are some new girls on the team this year . . . ?"

"But, Mom," Libby groaned, "you know I'm hor-r-r-r-rible at swimming—you know I said I was never ever, ever, ever going back to the swim team after last year."

Mrs. Thump was halfway up the stairs and said over her shoulder, "You never know, Libby, you might be better than you think you are. But at the very least you would be helping a friend—Suzanne says that Brittany is just not herself."

"Do you believe that?" Libby said to Margaret, and the dog wagged her tail. Libby fed her a handful of Cheerios and tried to picture this new Just Not Herself Brittany. Did Brittany really miss her? If Libby thought about it, did she miss Brittany—maybe just a little? They used to play together all the time . . . what had happened?

Realizing that resistance was futile, Libby arrived at the pool in her regulation beach club swim team bathing suit an hour later with an open mind toward Brittany. There was no mistaking Brittany even through the swarm of kids in the same outfit. She was by the edge of the pool, joking and laughing, the center of attention, surrounded by a group of six girls. She looked like she had plenty of friends.

Libby knew everybody because practically every kid in Mrs. Williams's class went to the beach club. Mim was there and Libby hurried over, but it was plain to see that Just Not Herself Brittany was just exactly like herself.

"Where are the new girls?" Libby asked, expecting them to be a figment of her mother's imagination as well. Brittany nodded over to a group of girls who were trying to push one another into the water. They were taller than Libby and looked older.

"They're really fast." Mim sounded a little worried.

The coach blew his whistle. Up and down the pool Libby clung to her kickboard. The new girls zoomed

past her, and in their wake Brittany followed, kicking furiously. But there was no catching the new girls; they *were* fast and glided through the water like a school of dolphins.

Meanwhile, everything Libby disliked about swim practice was coming back to haunt her—the smell of the chlorine, the water in her ears, the water in her mouth when she was trying to breathe, the coach

yelling at her to go faster, and how everyone seemed faster than she would ever be.

"You'll get better," Mim said optimistically when it was all over.

But Libby wasn't so sure.

The two girls headed to the beach to dry off. As they left the pool, Libby spotted her sister. She was still in her riding clothes.

"Hey . . ." Libby waved to get her attention and was about to call out. She was eager to hear how the lesson went, but Laurel was talking to some boy as she played with her hair and giggled.

"What's she doing?" Libby said. Laurel hardly ever smiled, let alone giggled!

"She's flirting!" Mim snickered.

"Come on," Libby said. "Let's go." There was something more than a little embarrassing about the way her sister was acting, and Libby didn't want Laurel to know she had just seen it for herself.

10
LAUREL'S NEWS

That night at the dinner table Laurel had something to tell everyone. "Guess what?"

Libby held her breath. These days Libby never
knew what Laurel would do next. What was she going
to say? "Hey, everybody, I've got a boyfriend?"

But Laurel had something even more surprising to
announce.

"I'm going to be in a horse show!"

"What?" Had Libby heard right?

"In two weeks," Laurel said proudly.

Libby wasn't the only one in the family who was surprised.

Her father's fork was poised in midair two inches from his mouth and a piece of lettuce teetered, fell off, and plopped back onto the dish. "But you've only ridden a few times."

"That's fantastic, honey!" Mrs. Thump was always all for anything competitive.

"It's just a walk/trot class," Laurel said, trying to downplay her role. "Emily is going to ride Benson—"

"*Emily's* going to a show?" Libby interrupted. Had Emily actually listened to her? Libby was amazed. This was a first—no one *ever* listened to her!

Laurel continued, "Emily said I could come to the show and ride in a class if . . ."

"If what?" Mrs. Thump paused from her meal, which she had been eating with gusto.

"You need the right clothes to be in a horse show. Emily said she would let me borrow a pair of her britches, and a shirt and jacket, but . . ." Laurel looked down self-consciously at her plate. "Emily doesn't have a pair of riding boots that would fit me."

No one said a word and all you could hear were crickets. Libby didn't know how much riding boots cost, but she knew that her father's landscaping business was not doing well. Lately there had been fewer customers.

"How much are these boots?" her father wanted to know.

"I—I don't know," Laurel said softly.

Mrs. Thump patted Laurel's hand. "We'll find a way," she said reassuringly, and glanced at her husband.

"You will?" Laurel said hopefully.

Mr. Thump frowned. "People are cutting their own lawns nowadays." No one said a thing and Mr. Thump laughed to lighten the mood. "Worst comes to worst, we'll set you up with a lemonade stand out on the front lawn, Laurel."

Libby looked from her mother to her father to Laurel, wondering what that meant. Would Laurel or wouldn't Laurel get riding boots? But for the moment the subject appeared to be closed.

Later that night Libby shoved at the sleeping Margaret, who, as usual, was taking up the whole bed. Finally comfortable, she was just about to fall asleep when her ears pricked up. Had she just heard her name? It was extremely interesting to hear her name, and Libby jumped out of bed to listen from her door. Light filtered out from her parents' room and snippets of a conversation between them floated down the darkened hall.

". . . Libby is so interested in drawing and she loves horses," her mother was saying.

"I know," her father said. "You mark my words—that girl is going to go far in life."

"But I worry about Laurel . . . ," Mrs. Thump continued. "Up till now she hasn't found anything that she really likes to do. . . ."

"She likes to text her friends," her father chuckled. "Does that count as an interest?"

"I know, but it seems like she's a pretty good

rider—otherwise Emily wouldn't have suggested the show."

"But if we had any extra money right now, we'd have allowed Libby to take lessons too," her father said.

"I feel so badly about that." Her mother sighed. "It was a hard call."

"I guess," her father said. "I just wish . . ."

Suddenly the door closed and Libby ducked back into her room.

". . . can't afford—not now." Her father was saying something, but she couldn't hear very well now.

Then there was silence. Libby tiptoed back to bed. She couldn't stop thinking about what her father had said; she was going to go far in life! She—Libby Thump—was GOING TO GO FAR IN LIFE! But how did he know? She strained her ears to listen again. Would they say any more?

She waited for fifteen minutes, but there was only the sound of Margaret's steady breathing. Her parents had said that before Laurel started taking riding lessons, she didn't have any other interests besides her friends. Libby thought about it and they were right, but so what?

Libby lay on her side and stroked Margaret, who snored quietly. Libby still didn't think Laurel should even get riding lessons—much less boots. She couldn't help it, though, she was starting to feel sort of sorry for Laurel—she had been so excited about being in a show and now it wasn't going to happen—but Libby felt even worse for her mother and father. She knew they wished they could just give Laurel the money for the boots—as well as the money for Libby's riding lessons too.

If only she had some money, she could buy her own lessons. Maybe a lemonade stand wasn't such a bad idea. . . . How many glasses of lemonade would you have to sell, though? It made her sleepy just thinking about it . . . seemed like it would take forever.

Wait a minute. Libby sat bolt upright. Emily had said that she and Sal barely had the time to take care of the horses, let alone train seriously. . . . What if she helped out at High Hopes Horse Farm? What if she got paid? Then she could buy lessons! What a great idea! Libby got under the covers so that she could fall asleep quickly, so that it could hurry up and be morning, so that she could Go Far in Life.

When Libby woke, she dressed quickly and ran downstairs. It was a dismal scene in the kitchen that greeted her. Mrs. Thump stood at the counter watching Laurel, who sat gloomily at the table before a plate of eggs that she hadn't touched. Mr. Thump held a cup of coffee in one hand and a stack of bills in the other.

"There'll be other shows, honey," Mrs. Thump said sympathetically, and exchanged looks with Mr. Thump, who looked on helplessly.

Libby slid into her chair and grinned; she couldn't wait to tell everyone. "I'm going to get a job!" she announced.

"A job?!" her mother and her father both said, surprised. Laurel looked up, interested.

"Yep! Emily and Sal need help, and I'm going to

work at High Hopes Horse Farm to make money to pay for my lessons!"

"That's a great idea, Lib, but you're only ten years old," Libby's father said.

"Going on eleven," Libby reminded him.

"But don't you think that if Sal and Emily had the money, they would hire help?" Mrs. Thump said gently.

Laurel, who had been glum only a minute ago, was now busting to be heard. "What about me?" She was out of her chair. "Maybe *I* could work there in *exchange* for lessons—then I could buy my boots!"

It was happening AGAIN! Libby couldn't believe it! "But I can work as good as Laurel!"

"You've got a whole lifetime to work, kid," her father laughed, and waved his stack of bills.

That afternoon Libby didn't get a job at High Hopes Horse Farm—but Laurel did.

For now Libby was going to have to wait to Go Far in Life.

No. It wasn't fair.

11

LIBBY'S BACK!

The week leading up to riding lesson day felt like it took a million years. Libby had to find ways to keep herself busy, so when Mim invited her to watch ballet class, Libby jumped at the chance.

Mim looked so pretty! She was wearing a pale pink leotard with white tights and white ballet slippers. Her hair was pulled up into a bun and tied with a pink ribbon.

Libby and Mim's mother, along with several other

parents, sat on folding chairs off to the side. They were in a room with wood flooring and long metal bars secured to the walls. Above hung framed pictures of ballerinas in pink tutus, and Libby thought that Mim looked just like them! About a dozen girls lined up next to Mim at the bar. A hush fell over the room when the teacher entered. She was a stern older woman in black tights and a flowing sweater, her hair pulled severely back from her face and twisted into a knot at the back of her head. The woman nodded and a young man who was sitting at a piano off in the corner began to play.

"First position!" the teacher ordered, and the girls got into a pose with their feet pointed out. Libby had never seen her friend so serious! There was second and third position after that. They went through all the positions—the hardest, Libby thought, was fifth position, which ended up with the feet turned in opposite directions. "Demi-plié!" the teacher said. The girls bent their knees, then straightened their legs.

They added the arms, which dipped down and then swooped in an arc up over their heads.

But the longer Libby watched, the more she became aware that something was not quite right. Was Mim's back not as straight as the other girls'? Did she wobble when she stood on one leg? Was she a little off kilter? Libby wasn't sure—she had never been to a ballet class before. But Mim had—she went all the time. How could Mim not be the best in the class by now? Libby wanted Mim to be the best in the class. She watched some more.

After a while the girls left the bar and performed a dance. The class glided and turned across the floor as a group, but Mim was having trouble keeping up. She was two steps behind the other girls and noticeably out of time.

The music stopped. "And rest," the teacher said.

Libby couldn't help feeling disappointed for Mim because of the way she had danced. But Mim didn't seem to mind. She didn't have a care in the world. Her eyes glittered with exhilaration and her mother gave her a hug.

"That was fun," Libby said when they dropped her off at home. "Thanks for letting me come." Mim waved from the car as they drove away.

Libby sat down on her front lawn and lay back. She looked up at the clouds. Mim was her best friend, but there was no denying it: Mim stank at ballet! Mim stank at ballet as bad as Libby stank at swimming. The difference was that it didn't bother Mim. Libby couldn't understand. Why would Mim keep trying to do something that she had absolutely no talent for?

Tomorrow Libby would be going back to the barn. She couldn't wait to ride Cough Drop. She couldn't wait to learn how to groom Princess and make her beautiful again just like she was in the photographs in the tack room. And she couldn't wait to be the Best Rider in the Entire World, just like Emily.

Libby wondered: Her father had predicted that she would Go Far in Life; would it be as a rider? Would she get first place in a horse show someday? Would she ever be able to jump gigantic fences like Emily? Maybe even get on the equestrian team and go to the Olympics? Why not? Right now anything was possible! Right now there was potential—and Libby would do everything she could to live up to it!

Libby lay on the grass and waited for Laurel's return. Laurel had gone to the barn every day to get ready for the horse show. Libby's only way of knowing what was going on at High Hopes Horse Farm was through any news she could worm out of her sister.

"How's the barn?" Libby asked when Laurel finally got home.

Laurel checked her phone for messages and answered without stopping, "Fine."

Libby followed her sister. "What'd you do?"

"Rode Summer . . ."

"D'you canter?"

"Yes."

"D'you jump?"

Laurel kept walking and texting on her way to her room.

"D'you jump?"

At dinner Laurel was more conversational. "Sal got a new horse today."

Libby looked up.

"He's right off the racetrack and Emily says he's crazy! Name's Ghost." Laurel took a big bite out of her ear of corn.

"Weird name," Libby said, and took a big bite out of her ear of corn.

"It's a nickname they gave him because the horse shies so much they think he sees ghosts all the time," Laurel said.

"Shies? What's that?" Mrs. Thump asked.

"It means he jumps and is startled at every little thing he sees," Laurel replied.

"Yeah, like every little blade of grass," Libby added. "Has Emily ridden him yet, Laurel?"

"Nope."

"Sal?"

"Sal's been in a bad mood—not happy 'bout the show."

"Oh." Libby drew down her upper lip and was quiet. Libby remembered how it was *her* idea for Emily to start showing again.

That night Libby worried about Sal. Why was he not happy about the horse show? Was he mad at her for suggesting it? Most of all Libby didn't want that.

By morning Libby was still worried.

Laurel had been walking to the barn these days, and Libby cantered ahead through the park. Out of the woods they came and squeezed in between the rails of the old splintered fence. Princess grazed peacefully out in the pasture.

"Hello, Princess!" Libby called, and the horse raised her head.

Down in the barn everything looked the same—only neater. Having Laurel there seemed to make a difference. The aisle was swept and some of the clutter was gone from in front of the stalls. But as usual old General George's lower lip hung down well below the upper and his eyes were half closed. Libby kissed his nose and he opened his eyes.

She looked in on Cough Drop, who came right over to her, ears forward and all smiles. But as soon as he could see there were no carrots, he rudely turned his rump to Libby and ate his hay.

"I'm back!" she called to Emily. "Are you excited about the show?"

Emily was coming toward her. "I am, but Sal's not."

So Sal really *was* unhappy about Emily going to a horse show. Libby shuffled her feet nervously and changed the subject. "Where's the new horse?"

"Third stall down—don't know why Sal took 'im," Emily said irritably. "Last thing we need around here's another horse!"

As soon as Libby got close, the new horse flattened his ears and gave her a dirty look. He was black as a crow, with no white markings. When Cough Drop was all tacked up, Libby led him down the aisle and Ghost glared at them from his corner as they passed. Libby decided she would keep her distance from this horse.

Out in the ring Emily gave Laurel her lesson this day. Libby could see how much Laurel had improved over the last two weeks. She had her long blond hair in one thick braid that swung back and forth in time to the trot. Emily had lent her a pair of breeches and Laurel was starting to look like a real rider now!

Libby thought about wearing her hair in one long braid down her back. She wished Emily would lend her a pair of breeches. She listened harder than ever to catch everything Emily was telling Laurel. Look up, hands together, heels down, legs back, elbows at her sides—it was a lot to remember. She knew it would be a whole lot easier if only she had Emily correcting her position like Laurel did.

Libby tried trotting Cough Drop and was just starting to get the hang of posting when Sal led Ghost out of the barn. He was tacked up and jigging nervously. The hair on his neck was already starting to darken with sweat.

Libby stopped to watch.

Sal stood on the mounting block. "Easy, easy," he tried to calm the horse. Ghost pulled his tail under him and shied, pulling Sal off the block.

Emily was watching too and shouted, "Sal! Your leg! You'll get hurt! Let me help you!"

Sal's face was tense with concentration focused only on the horse. He limped over to the mounting block again, pulling the horse with him, and got him to stand. But as soon as his foot was in the stirrup, Ghost moved and Sal had barely enough time to swing his right leg over the saddle.

The horse reared, showing the whites of his eyes.

"Be careful!" Libby cried. Emily was frozen in place.

Sal leaned forward and Ghost put his head down between his front legs. He rounded his back and Sal

kicked him. The horse grunted and all four legs came off the ground. He landed and dropped his left shoulder. Sal's right leg came out of the stirrup and he fell on the ground still holding the reins. Emily ran over, but Sal was already standing.

Back at the mounting block Sal laid a hand gently against the horse's neck to calm him. "It's all right then, all right." He was able to get on this time without mishap and rode Ghost down the drive. The horse threw his head and spooked all the way.

"Sal!" Emily called. But Sal and Ghost had disappeared over the hill. For the rest of Laurel's lesson Emily was quiet.

Afterward she was subdued on the way out to Princess's paddock. She carried a halter with a lead and a bucket filled with grooming equipment. Libby followed silently.

Emily curried one portion of Princess and then demonstrated how to brush, leaving the rest of the mare for Libby to do. Twelve inches were cut off Princess's tail, and the knots were combed out of her mane.

Libby could tell that Emily was in no mood for conversation this day, but she had to ask.

"Is Sal mad at me, Emily?" Libby asked softly.

"No. He's mad at me," Emily said.

Off in the distance they could see Sal and Ghost on their way home. The horse pranced and zigzagged across the field. Emily shook her head.

"That horse looks mad too," Libby remarked.

"He's not mad—he's scared."

"Scared of what?"

"Of being hurt, most likely," Emily said. "I saw a guy I worked for years ago spend an hour trying to catch a horse in a field, and soon as he caught him, he yanked on the lead and yelled at the horse."

"That's horrible!" Libby cried.

"And the guy was a really good rider—one of the best in the country."

"How can that be?" Libby was horrified.

"Just because a person's good at something doesn't

make him a good person, Libby—you'll find that out soon enough."

She watched Emily leave and Libby felt anxious. No matter what Emily said, Sal was not happy about her going to the show and that was Libby's fault.

Sal and Ghost came up the driveway. She could see him rub the crest of the horse's mane. Ghost stretched out his neck and finally stopped jigging. Emily had said that Ghost wasn't mad—he was just scared. Libby wondered if the same went for Sal. Could it be that Sal wasn't mad about Emily going off to a horse show—could it be that he was scared?

12

SLEEPING BEAUTY

It was the week leading up to the show, and wild horses couldn't keep Libby away from High Hopes Horse Farm.

Laurel got to ride Summer every day in return for cleaning stalls.

"I can clean stalls too," Libby told Sal.

"Got enough stall cleaners for the time being." Sal was sweeping the aisle and Libby followed behind.

Through the door to the tack room Libby could see the two cleaning hooks groaning under the weight of a tangle of dirty bridles.

"I could clean tack!" Libby said as helpfully as she could.

Sal swept a pile of manure and shavings onto a shovel and dumped it all in a muck basket. "You want to do tack?"

"More than anything in the world!" Libby said.

They went into the tack room and Sal picked up a sponge in each hand. "First wipe the bridles off with warm water using this sponge, then go over them again using Lexol and saddle soap on this sponge—and don't mix up the sponges."

"I won't, Sal, I promise." Libby took the precious sponges. The saddle soap sponge felt sticky.

"And take the bits off the bridles, wash 'em in soapy water, and put 'em back on."

"Bits off."

"And put the bits back on the correct bridles."

"Bits on the correct bridles." Libby saluted. "I'll do a really good job—you'll see!"

All morning Libby feverishly cleaned tack. By noon she had all the bridles done and you could see the cleaning hooks for the first time in months.

She wished that she could show Sal all her hard work, but he was out on the tractor in a far paddock.

In the ring Emily rode a young horse that she was teaching how to jump. Laurel set poles on the ground and some cross rails.

"Need any help?" Libby shouted to her sister.

"No, we're good," Laurel said.

"You eating lunch soon?" Libby asked.

"In a while," Laurel called back.

"Move the poles a little closer," Emily instructed Laurel.

Everybody was busy except Libby. With nothing to do, she wandered back and headed for the tack room. She sat down heavily on a trunk and stared at her sandwich with very little appetite. She had been riding Cough Drop as perfectly as she could. She had been watching and listening to every single thing that Sal and Emily told Laurel to do. She had learned how to groom Princess. She had even given Laurel the idea for how to get a job and pay for her stupid boots! And where did it get her? Sal didn't care about all the tack she had just done, and now Laurel and Emily were best friends and she was sitting here all alone.

No. It wasn't fair.

Her eyes went to the photos on the wall. The dusty pictures were mostly of Princess and Sal jumping huge fences at horse shows, but in one she stood with a ribbon on her bridle. Libby took it from the wall and wiped it off so that she could study it. Princess had her mane braided and stood proudly. Her coat was sleek and shiny.

Libby left her lunch but took the apple she had brought for dessert. She got the bucket with the brushes, along with a big sponge and some shampoo.

Princess dozed out of the noonday heat in her dilapidated shed. One hind leg bent, she stood on a patch of mud that had dried into a rock-hard pattern of hoofprints. Her head was lowered and flies collected around her face. It was such a sad ending to the story the pictures in the tack room told. Libby knew just how Princess felt, stuck out in some field, all alone, forgotten.

Libby's approach roused the mare from her slumber. She nickered at Libby as if to say hello. She didn't have a swayback like General George or grass belly like Cough Drop. Under all that dirt and hair the champion jumper—the old Princess—slept. Libby could see she was still a beauty.

Libby waved the flies away from Princess's face and gave her the apple.

She had seen Emily bathe Cough Drop, and now she got to work on Princess. From her neck to her rump white suds turned brown from dirt. Libby shampooed her mane and tail and then used buckets and buckets of water from the pump to rinse her off.

A veteran of thousands of baths in her lifetime, Princess stood quietly without having to be tied. Libby scraped the excess water off the horse's back and sides. Then she rubbed her down with a towel and dried her legs and fetlocks just like she'd seen Emily do.

By the time she finished bathing Princess, Libby was a mess. Dirt and hay clung to her shoes. Her jeans had two brown knee stains from kneeling in the paddock, and were so bagged out she could hardly keep them up. Her braids were dusty and she was sweaty. But Princess was gorgeous! As her coat dried, Libby couldn't believe what a difference a bath could make—she looked like a new horse! And Libby couldn't have been happier.

Libby unbuckled the mare's halter and hung it on a post by the gate. Princess followed by her side. Libby stopped. Princess stopped. Libby walked and Princess walked. Libby turned to the right and Princess turned to the right too. It was as if she were tethered to the lead rope—but she wasn't. Princess was following Libby better than Margaret ever had!

"Good girl!" Libby laughed. She dumped the mare's dirty water buckets and filled them with fresh water. Libby neatly piled the hay that had been scattered about the shed. All the while Princess followed Libby around the paddock like an overgrown dog.

Finally it was time for Libby to go. "I'll be back tomorrow," Libby promised. Princess hung her head over the fence and watched the girl run across the pasture until she disappeared from sight through the fence and into the woods.

13
DARK CLOUDS OVER HIGH HOPES

The next day something was wrong at High Hopes Horse Farm. Libby could feel it the minute she walked into the barn. Emily passed her leading Benson without saying hello, and Sal was even more quiet than usual. Libby and Laurel got their horses, and since nobody offered, the girls tacked them up themselves.

"Girth's on wrong," Sal mumbled.

He unbuckled Cough Drop's girth and turned it around. "Folded part goes next to the elbow."

Libby thanked Sal, but he didn't answer.

Inside the ring Emily circled at the walk on Benson in front of the gate. "Libby, see if Sal is coming out— he's supposed to help me school for the show," she grumbled.

But when Libby got to the barn, Sal was on his way out on Ghost. "Emily needs your help, Sal."

"No, she doesn't." Skittish as usual, Ghost side-stepped an old plastic bag that lay in the weeds and shied at a rock. Unfazed, Sal rode off down the drive.

"Sal!" Emily called. He acted like he hadn't heard, and Emily looked like she was going to cry.

Laurel sat on Summer. "Emily—he'll be back."

"But I need someone to set up a fence!"

"We can do that!" Libby said.

Emily took a deep breath and collected herself. Libby and Laurel got off their horses and set up a wide fence, called an oxer, with three striped rails in the front and a higher rail behind it.

"Higher," Emily said.

"Really?" Laurel and Libby hesitated. They raised it till it was almost as high as Libby's head.

Emily started to trot over smaller jumps, but she was clearly off. Benson put in some extra strides and Emily got left behind, her legs out in front of her. She picked up a canter and Benson became strong and rushed at the gate fence, knocking down the top rail. Libby and Laurel ran over to replace it.

Emily pulled Benson up sharply and cantered and stopped, cantered and stopped, until he seemed more under control. But when she started a small course, he was taking off way too soon from the jumps.

Libby held her breath. So far Emily had avoided the big oxer, but now she was headed right for it. She looked all wrong going in—her reins were long and Benson was going too fast. A second before he was supposed to take off, he threw his legs out in front

of him and skidded into the fence. Emily was pitched
forward and almost came off—rails went flying. The
girls quickly put the fence back up. Emily kicked
Benson hard and switched her crop to the other hand.
She cantered around, holding him tightly.

Benson was very upset. White foam flew off in long

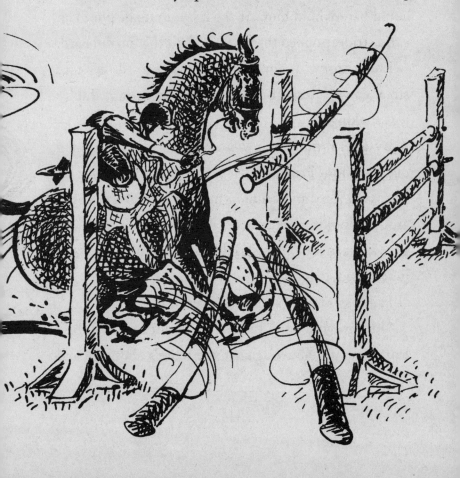

strings from his mouth, and there was lather on his sides behind her leg—he was covered in sweat. She jumped him over the brush box and then pulled him into a tight canter. She headed him toward the oxer again, and he hopped up and down like a rocking horse—then a few strides away he shot ahead. Emily looked like she could barely hold him. At the last minute he put in an extra stride, popped the fence, and hit the top rail hard.

Emily threw down her reins and walked, her face streaked with tears. Benson was blowing hard. Libby was shaking.

By afternoon clouds were forming. Libby headed out to groom Princess. The mare nickered as soon as she saw Libby and came right over to her. She nosed around, looking for treats. Libby broke a carrot and gave her a piece. "You should be glad you're out here in the shed, Princess."

Princess snorted and shook her head.

"I know, you don't believe me, but it's true." Libby leaned on an elbow against the mare's shoulder and ate a carrot too. "You see, Emily's taking Benson to a horse show, and Sal's mad, and then Emily got mad, and now they're both mad at each other. And Benson jumped horribly—and the show's in only three days." Libby fed the thick end of her carrot to Princess. "And the worst part is that I think it's all my fault."

Princess gave her a baleful look and Libby sighed. Today she wanted to try pulling Princess's mane. Emily had shown her how on Cough Drop. With a metal mane comb she had teased a section of the pony's mane. She had wrapped the remainder of the hair in her fingers around the comb and pulled.

"Ow!" Libby had flinched. "It looks like it hurts."

"In the beginning sometimes it does, but horses get used to it. Not too short on Princess, mind you," Emily had warned. "She needs the hair as protection against the flies this summer."

Libby turned a bucket over and stood on it to reach Princess's mane, then paused. Libby was nervous— it seemed like it *would* hurt—but when she started,

Princess didn't seem to mind. In a short while the ground was covered in long white hair.

Princess was perfect now. Her mane was even, and her tail was cut straight across at the hocks. The dirt and matted hair was gone. But as Libby stood admiring her work, she could feel a cool breeze and the wind was kicking up. The sun had gone in. Libby gathered her grooming tools, and Princess followed her to the gate. She sniffed Libby's pockets and hands. "Which one?" Libby asked. She held a piece of carrot in one fist. But Princess knew that game. She nudged Libby's hand and Libby gave her the treat.

It was time to go. She snapped the gate shut. The mare hung her head over the fence. "Maybe Sal and Emily have made up by now," Libby hoped aloud as she stroked the mare's nose.

But the mood was still somber back in the barn. Libby was glad to see that at least someone was happy.

"This is for you!" Mr. McClave handed her a large envelope and she knew exactly what it was.

"General George from the good old days!" Libby exclaimed.

The horse was in a grassy field surrounded by a dozen hounds. Gone was the swayback and the hollows above his eyes. His ears were pricked and he was looking intelligently off into the distance. His coat had been clipped, giving it a suede appearance, with his legs outlined in the hair that had been left there. Mr. McClave sat tall, his shoulders squared in his red jacket—a jaunty smile shone from under the brim of his black velvet riding cap.

Libby was awed. "Can I keep it for a while—to draw from?"

"You may keep it as long as you like, my dear." Mr. McClave laughed softly. "I expect a great work of art!"

George whinnied from his stall. "If you'll excuse me, George and I have some catching up to do." Mr. McClave gave Libby a wink and was gone.

Laurel told Libby they would be picked up soon. Libby could see Emily alone in the tack room cleaning her saddle. Sal, his hands jammed into his pockets, his eyes on the ground, limped out to a pasture to bring in some horses. Libby waited by the front door of the barn and couldn't help noticing the sky was slate gray and dark clouds hung low over High Hopes Horse Farm.

14

JUST NOT HERSELF LIBBY

The next day when Libby woke up, she found out that Laurel wasn't going over to the barn. That meant that neither was Libby.

Libby was just not herself.

She sat at the breakfast table, chin in her hand, pushing her cereal around in the bowl.

Laurel sat in her shorts with her bare feet up on the chair next to her. Her head bent forward, she scanned her phone for messages behind a curtain of blond hair.

"But *why* aren't you going?" Libby said impatiently.

Laurel's eyes were glued to her phone. "Shush already."

"But the show is two days away!" Libby said desperately. "You need to practice, and get Summer ready, and clean your tack, and all sorts of stuff!"

"I'm going over to the barn later, all right?" As Laurel left the room, she gathered her hair up into a ponytail and twisted it around and around in her hand until it was tightly wound and then let it go. Libby rolled her eyes.

Mrs. Thump came over with her coffee and sat in Laurel's empty chair. She leaned toward Libby. "Suzanne says Brittany's outfit is going to be so cute! We need to get your best princess attire together today."

Libby put her spoon down and switched her chin to her other hand.

"I guess," she said glumly.

Mrs. Thump took a big gulp of coffee. "Suzanne picked up a little rhinestone tiara, and she had a dressmaker whip up a full skirt all in different shades of pink!"

Libby gave her mother a weak smile.

Her mother rattled on, "There're sequins and bows and little plastic roses! I can't wait to see it—can you?!"

Actually, Libby could wait and wished her mother would show the same excitement about High Hopes Horse Farm.

"So what do you say?"

"About what?"

"We could look through some of your old dress-up clothes?" Mrs. Thump said breezily. And then the lack of enthusiasm gave her another idea. "I've got an old bridesmaid's dress from college that we can use, and we'll put some sweet little bows and dried flowers on it—it'll look awesome!"

Libby hated it when her mother used words like "awesome."

By afternoon Libby stood in front of her mother's full-length mirror in a cutoff bridesmaid's dress with sweet little bows and dried flowers.

Mrs. Thump had her phone poised—she couldn't wait to call Suzanne.

"You look awesome, honey!" Mrs. Thump exclaimed.

Libby cringed. "But, Mom, don't you think I'm a little too old for all this princess stuff?"

"Too old? Libby, you're ten, for heaven's sake!"

"I'll be eleven in a month and a half," Libby said impatiently—she wished she didn't have to keep reminding everybody of this!

Mrs. Thump started dialing. "You're not too old— Suzanne? Remember that old bridesmaid's dress from my college roommate's wedding?"

Margaret stood outside Mrs. Thump's room and stared at Libby suspiciously.

"It's okay, girl," Libby said. "It's still me."

Unconvinced, Margaret barked at her.

Suddenly Libby became aware of how hot the dress made her. She fumbled with the zipper and finally peeled it off her damp skin.

Outside the air was heavy and the sky overcast. The next day was swim practice.

"Maybe there'll be a big storm and it'll get canceled, Margaret," Libby said hopefully. But by the next morning conditions were still the same. The heat was oppressive and the sky was dark, but still no rain.

The whistle blew and Libby held on for dear life to the side of the pool. She tried to catch her breath and get the water out of her eyes so she could see. Now the coach was telling Libby to get out of the pool because they were supposed to break up into two groups to swim a relay race.

Libby sloshed over to Brittany to be on her team.

"There's no room on our team." Brittany pointed. "You can swim on *that* team."

"*That* team?" Libby didn't want to swim on *that* team because it was the scary-fast new girls' team.

Libby's shoulders sagged.

It was all over in under ten minutes. By the time Libby made it across the pool, the scary-fast new girls had lost the relay.

Libby dried off and Mim came over to console her. "You'll get faster when you've had more practice." But that didn't make her feel any better.

Libby, Mim, and Brittany left the pool together, and Libby wasn't talking—that is, until Brittany said, "I hear your sister is taking riding lessons."

"Yes, she is—and I am too," said Libby. "I'm even going to be in a horse show tomorrow!"

"You are?" Brittany was impressed.

"Yes, I've got real riding pants and tall black boots—and I'm riding a white horse who used to be a champion show jumper."

"Wow!" said Mim.

"Can I come and watch?" Brittany sounded excited.

"Probably not," Libby said. "I think it's three states away."

"Wow!" both girls said. They had reached Brittany's locker and she paused. "I hope you'll be back in time for my party. . . ."

"Oh yeah." Libby waved one hand assuredly. "I'll be back in plenty of time."

Libby and Mim went down to the sand to sit on their beach towels and dry off.

They passed Mrs. Williams, who sat under an umbrella. She glanced up from her book and looked at the girls firmly. Libby immediately felt guilty for saying those things to Brittany.

Mim was talking. "That's so great—you're going to be in a horse show tomorrow, Libby!"

"I'm not going to be in a horse show." Libby didn't look at Mim when she spoke.

"But why—"

"I'm not even taking riding lessons." Libby threw her towel on the sand and sat.

"So why'd you say all that to Brittany?" Mim asked her friend.

Libby explained to Mim all about Just Not Herself Brittany.

"It's sort of true . . . ," Mim said thoughtfully. "Brittany's always been the best one on the team, until these new girls came. The coach spends a lot of time with them and I think Brittany's been upset."

"She should be happy now—her team beat them thanks to me," Libby said sharply.

"Do you think Brittany will tell her mom?" Mim asked finally.

"Probably." Libby didn't want to think what would happen then.

Down the beach next to the jetty, away from the families and little kids, a boy and girl sat on a beach blanket together.

Mim pointed. "Those two look like they're going to start kissing!"

The girl swept up her hair into a ponytail and twisted it around and around before letting it fall.

Libby squinted to see and suddenly realized, "That's Laurel!"

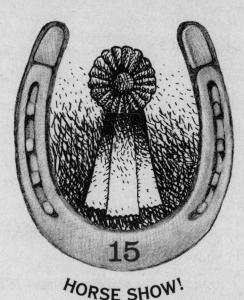

15

HORSE SHOW!

By evening the heat had become unbearable. Libby pushed her hair out of her face and it felt frizzy with humidity—not even like her normal hair. Margaret lay flat on her tummy on the tiles in the hall, trying to stay cool.

Laurel and Libby set the table for dinner.

"So," Libby said casually, "who's your boyfriend?"

Laurel glanced at her sister, but Libby never looked up.

"What?" Laurel went to the silverware drawer.

"The beach today? You? Sitting on the beach towel *with* . . . ?" Libby stood holding four glasses and looked at her sister questioningly.

"He's not my *boyfriend*." Laurel tossed her head. "He's just some kid."

Laurel noisily grabbed a handful of knives, forks, and spoons. "Seriously," she muttered.

Libby backed off and changed the subject. "I can't wait for the show tomorrow."

"Yeah, I mean it's just a walk/trot class—it's not like I'm going to the Olympics."

"No, it's not," Libby agreed, but she thought it was kind of a weird thing to say. Libby was excited about the horse show and she wasn't even riding in it!

Later that night thunder rumbled and Margaret scooted under Libby's bed for protection.

Finally it had begun to rain, and Margaret was whining softly.

"Come on, girl." Libby leaned over the side of her bed and a nose poked out. The dog hopped up next to

Libby. She was trembling, and Libby curled her body around Margaret and petted her. "It's okay."

But Libby couldn't sleep. Her mom would soon hear from Brittany's mom all about how Libby had bragged she was going to be in a horse show. Listening to the rain, Libby worried about that, too. Tomorrow the ground would be slick, just like the day that Sal and Princess had their accident. Would Emily and Benson be all right?

There was a flash of lightning, then thunder, and the rain came down heavier now. Libby listened to the rain beat down and wished she hadn't encouraged Emily to go to this horse show. What if the same thing happened to her that happened to Sal and Princess? With all this on her mind it was difficult to sleep.

Libby woke up with a start. It was dark and she felt like she'd been asleep only a few minutes when she heard the car in the driveway. She peered out the window and saw the taillights disappear down the road. Her mother was taking Laurel to the barn. At least it had stopped raining, but Libby knew the footing would be slippery. She already had butterflies in her stomach just thinking about Emily jumping Benson today.

A few hours later Libby squished through the mud with her mother and father in between two big white tents held down with ropes and stakes. All around them horses and riders milled. The sky was still unsettled, the sides of the tents flapped, and some of the horses spooked as they passed.

There were a lot of girls of different ages leading, riding, and grazing their horses. Some were schooling in a separate ring off to the side that had just a few jumps set up in the middle. Their trainers busily lowered and raised fences as the girls went around and around, trotting and cantering over the jumps.

Parents and siblings stood by the schooling ring reading their programs and holding a variety of essentials—fly spray, crops, rub rags, hoof dressing. The air crackled with tension. Libby felt jittery for the girls who were competing.

Horse trailers were lined up against a split-rail fence on the other side of a dirt road. "There she is!" Libby cried. Laurel was on Summer, and Emily held on to the horse's bridle. Summer pranced nervously as she was led across the road. There were no signs of Sal.

Libby and her parents were near two rings with newly whitewashed fencing. "Is this where Laurel's class is?" Mrs. Thump leafed through her program.

Mr. Thump looked over his wife's shoulder at it. "This is her ring—she's the first class of the morning!"

A voice boomed over the loudspeaker and Summer danced sideways.

"Riders in Walk/Trot, please enter ring two! Ring two, please!"

Laurel looked wonderful in Emily's borrowed navy blue jacket and canary-colored breeches. It was only days before that she had bought her boots, and they gleamed. Summer looked like a different horse with her mane and tail braided. But she was acting like a different horse as well.

"Ring two! Please!" the announcer repeated. Summer reared, but Emily still had hold of the bridle. The horse obstinately put her head up and backed a few steps.

"OH! I wish that loudspeaker would stop!" Mrs. Thump said anxiously.

Laurel's lips were pressed together to form one thin line, and her face was a waxy white color. Emily let go of Summer at the ingate and Laurel was on her own.

"Hi, honey!" Mr. Thump called to her when she went by, but Laurel never looked. The horse leaped over a puddle and she teetered to one side.

The judge sauntered into the ring holding a clipboard and they shut the gate. But Summer would not quiet down. She held her tail high and wouldn't walk, snapping her knees while Laurel bounced. Emily came over and stood with Libby and her parents.

"Where's Sal?" Libby asked.

"Not coming" was all Emily said, and Libby knew better than to ask why.

Laurel went by and Summer's head was straight up

in the air, her nostrils flared. Emily said to her in a low voice, "Keep your hands down."

"This is awful!" Libby felt sorry for Laurel.

"It's a good experience," Emily replied. "Horses are unpredictable—got to learn to deal with it."

Everyone was walking except for Laurel and Summer. Libby noticed that all the other kids were so much younger than her sister. One girl on a chestnut pony had bright ribbons on her pigtails and looked like she was six years old.

"Trot, please! All trot!" the judge said.

They all trotted and Summer cantered.

"*Trot*, please," the judge said as Laurel cantered by. She managed to halt and then made Summer walk and then trot.

"Good," Emily sighed with relief.

The riders were asked to reverse, and with new confidence Laurel shortened her reins and got Summer to walk. She trotted when they asked her to trot as well.

"She's doing better," Mrs. Thump whispered.

But when the horses were asked to line up, Summer would not stand still.

"We have the results for Walk/Trot. . . . In first place . . . ," the announcer said.

When the number of the little girl on the chestnut pony was called in first place, a loud whoop exploded from about ten people at the far side of the ring. Laurel's number was never called. Libby felt bad for her sister.

"I think you did very well," Mrs. Thump said brightly, and Mr. Thump agreed.

Laurel made a face and jumped off the mare. "I couldn't do anything with her."

"You never know what to expect with horses," Emily said. "But it was a good experience for you." Laurel didn't look like she was so sure. Emily and Laurel led Summer back to the trailer. Benson was up next and Emily had to get him ready for his class.

Libby was allowed to stay and watch, but her parents went home.

"Sorry," Libby said, a little out of breath as she to jogged to keep up.

"No big deal," Laurel said, and looked straight ahead.

"You want me to come with you?" Libby asked.

"I'd rather be alone for a bit."

Libby understood.

But a little while later, when Libby went to get a hot dog, she spied her sister and she was not alone. There under one of the tents by the food stand Laurel sat with the same boy that she had been with at the beach. Libby could see now that he had light blond hair cut so close that he looked bald, and he was pudgy. Laurel laughed and played with her hair—she *was* flirting! Libby made a detour so Laurel wouldn't see her, but Libby had made up her mind about something: Her sister liked a dork!

Libby went over to the schooling ring, and Emily was already there with Benson. His mahogany coat shimmered and the braids showed off his muscled, arched neck. Emily definitely looked like the best rider at the show, Libby thought. She leaned against the rail and watched Emily trot over fences. Benson jumped easily, unbothered by the slick footing or the loudspeaker. His ears flicked back and forth; he was listening only to Emily. But a moment later Emily abruptly brought Benson down to a walk. Libby wondered why. Then she knew.

Out of the crowd a familiar figure limped toward the schooling ring. Sal had come after all! He had some fly spray and a rub rag, but Emily never looked in his direction or acknowledged his presence. She just walked around the ring. She had lost her composure and Libby started to worry.

Emily hadn't jumped anything higher than two feet, and Libby wondered if she was going to school Benson over some bigger fences before she faced him with a course of them. Sal stayed a few feet back from the ring, and Emily continued just to walk.

It was making her too nervous, so Libby went over

to the show ring, and Laurel joined her—by herself. A dozen horses had already jumped, and the fences looked high and difficult. Worse, there was a huge oxer just like the one Benson had refused a few days before.

"Sal's here." Libby nudged Laurel. He was coming toward the show ring, and Libby noticed there was something different about Sal today. He had the same hitch in his stride, but the frown that she'd gotten so used to was gone. The fly spray bottle swung easily from one hand, and the rub rag fluttered from the other. Sal looked happy! Clearly, this was where Sal Ricci belonged.

Libby turned back to the ring. Another horse started and her nerves tingled with excitement. By now the footing was like soup. The horse cantered with effort through the deep, wet sand, and all Libby could think of was the accident that Sal had had on Princess. Libby chewed the end of one braid. The horse got over the oxer but pulled down two rails.

Emily and Benson were standing at the ingate now, waiting for their turn.

The next horse jumping was a little, round chestnut; on him was a tall, thin woman. The horse tucked his feet under him and jumped well, but when he came around to the oxer, the woman spurred him on at a terrific speed and the horse ran out. She kicked the little horse hard and waved her crop at him, but on his second try he ducked his head at the last minute and swerved to the right. The crowd gasped as her foot came out of one stirrup and she was thrown forward, coming dangerously close to falling off. The woman shortened her reins and held him tightly for a final try. They cantered strongly at the fence. She looked determined not to let him run out this time! On the last stride, just as he was about to lift off the ground, he put on the brakes and hopped straight through the fence, breaking two rails.

"Thank you!" the judge called out.

The woman and the little horse had been eliminated.

The jump crew scurried over to set up the fence.

Libby's heart was pounding by the time Emily entered the ring. She walked Benson in a circle, waiting for the fence to be fixed. Libby didn't know how Emily could be so calm! Finally the judge nodded for her to begin.

She gathered up her reins. Benson shook his head and swished his tail when he picked up a canter. Emily stood in her stirrups as they rounded the corner. The first fence was an inviting brush box, and as soon as she pointed him toward it, he sped up.

"Slow down," Libby whispered.

Benson cleared it—but just barely. The next fence was a gate with a lot of flower boxes on the ground in front of it. Emily sat down and leaned back, and Benson did slow down. She turned across the diagonal. He pricked his ears and headed for a large in and out. He jumped in, took a stride, and was out—so far he had jumped clean.

He came around going the other direction, and

Libby held her breath—three more fences until the huge oxer. The course twisted and turned. Emily urged and checked him to get to each fence at just the right takeoff. But Benson was strong and pulled. He lunged at a plain rail fence and hit it. The top rail came down—he was too fast and had flattened out. He would never make it over the oxer jumping like that.

Emily went around the corner toward it and Benson's head came up. Libby held on to her sister's arm, but two strides away Emily made a turn, circling in front of the fence.

"Counted as a refusal," a voice in the crowd said.

"Who is that riding?" another replied.

"She was a great rider—married Sal Ricci."

"Thought I heard he got hurt real bad."

"Yeah, he's finished."

"Shame."

The crowd murmured testily.

Emily halted Benson and then picked up a canter again. She circled in front of the oxer and a moment later headed straight for the huge fence. Libby gasped. One, two, three! He was up and over easily!

Libby started to breathe again—now only three more fences. But Emily brought Benson down to a walk and patted his neck loudly.

"She has more fences!" Libby didn't understand—why was Emily stopping?

Emily was eliminated for not finishing the course. There would be no ribbon for Benson today. But it didn't seem to matter. She praised him as she left the ring.

Libby and Laurel ran right over to her. Laurel held Benson while Emily loosened his girth.

"You did really good, Emily—but why didn't you finish the course?" Libby asked.

"I let him down last week, Libby," Emily replied. "I was upset and I shouldn't have been schooling him. He jumped the oxer perfectly and that's all I'm going to ask of him for today."

Sal came over and touched Emily lightly on her back. "You rode really well in there."

Emily gave Benson a lump of sugar.

"I'm sorry, Emily," Sal said almost inaudibly.

"He has potential, Sal," Emily said with conviction. "Benson deserves a chance—I want him to go as far as he can. . . ."

"So do I." Sal put her stirrups up. "I've been so caught up in feeling like this is the end for me . . . that . . . I don't know. . . ." His voice trailed off.

"It's not the end, Sal," Emily said more gently. "It's a new beginning."

"Hey, Sal!" A rider interrupted the conversation and slapped Sal on the back. "Where you been?"

They shook hands and started talking. A half a dozen other people came over as well, and soon Sal and Emily were surrounded by old friends.

"You still givin' lessons, Sal?" one of them asked.

Sal looked over at Libby and nodded. "Yeah, I'm still givin' lessons."

16

PRINCESS SPA PARTY

By the time Libby and Laurel got back to the barn, the first stars were coming out. The horses were all snug in their stalls, munching hay. Sal and Emily looked happier than they had in a while. High Hopes Horse Farm had gone to a show and not won a single ribbon, but everyone was content.

Libby had one more thing to do before she went home. The white mare stood patiently at her gate and waited. Libby needed to tell Princess about the show to let her know that everything had turned out fine. But that never happened.

Mrs. Thump drove up in the car. "I need to speak to you, Libby."

Libby gulped.

As soon as she got in the car, her mom said, "Did you tell Brittany that you were taking lessons and riding a champion jumper in a show that was three states away?"

"Sort of." Libby squirmed in her seat.

Laurel snorted and Mrs. Thump looked at Libby in the rearview mirror. "Why did you do that, Libby?"

"I don't know," Libby mumbled.

"That wasn't very nice—now Brittany thinks you're this big-time rider."

"She does?" Even if it wasn't true, it still gave Libby a lift to think that Brittany thought she was a "big-time rider."

"But, honey, you don't have to brag and try to be something you're not," her mother said.

When they got home, Libby hoped that the matter

would be dropped, like it never happened, but right away Mrs. Thump recounted the story and Mr. Thump listened closely.

"Libby, Libby, Libby," her dad said. He suppressed a laugh and strolled off to the other room. "Three states away?"

"I know," Libby said, embarrassed. "It's just that . . . Brittany thinks she's so big, and you said she was not herself, Mom—but she's just like herself. She's good at everything she does and she wouldn't let me be on her team for the relay and I had to swim on the scary-fast girls' team and I lost the whole relay and Brittany's team won and I hate swimming anyway—I have absolutely no potential as a swimmer. I want to ride— I want to be the best rider in the world, just like Emily. So that's why I told her all that stuff."

"I really think you should tell Brittany the truth tomorrow," her mother said.

"At the party?! Mom—NO WAY!" Libby was adamant.

"I don't know why you and Brittany can't be friends like when you were little girls." Her mother shook her head and followed her husband. "You adored each other."

Yeah, well, we don't now, Libby said to herself.

The next day Libby sat in the car in her mother's old, very pink bridesmaid's dress with the dried flowers and bows. Libby stared out the window and tried to make believe that she was on her way to somewhere else. Like, for instance, a horse show three states away to ride a champion jumper. She could hear the loudspeaker boom, "Our next rider is Libby Thump, riding Princess!"

The car stopped and Libby came out of her dream. There was a line of girls in pink leading into Brittany's house, and Libby glided in along with the others.

"I feel so stupid," Mim whispered.

"You too?" Libby said.

Inside, Brittany stood with her mother and greeted guests. Brittany was dressed head to toe in glitter and pink. Her long blond hair was piled on top of her head and anchored by a tiara. Her mother handed out little pink-and-gold gift bags. She was dressed as a waiter in black pants, a white top, and a bow tie. She even had a little white towel draped over one arm.

"Good afternoon, Princess Mim, Princess Libby." She bowed and handed them each a bag.

Brittany rolled her eyes.

"Happy birthday, Brittany," Libby mumbled.

"Thanks," Brittany mumbled back.

"That was weird," Mim whispered, and Libby agreed.

Libby and Mim were ushered out to the screened-in porch, which had been transformed into a princessy pink wonderland. The walls were covered with paper that had been painted to look like a castle. Big swaths of pink and gold cloth adorned the windows, as well as a long table laden with trays of pink sugared cupcakes, cookies, and candies. Pink and gold balloons stuck to the ceiling.

In each corner was stationed a "lady-in-waiting" to do the girls' nails, hair, and makeup. There was even a photographer to get a glamour shot of the final makeover.

"Cupcakes," Libby and Mim both said.

Libby had completely forgotten about the confession that her mother wanted her to make. She and Mim were trying to decide between the chocolate cupcakes with the pink frosting and the pink cupcakes with the chocolate frosting when suddenly Mrs. Thump stood before them holding Brittany's hand.

"Libby has something to say to you, dear. Libby?"

"I, um . . . like your outfit, Brittany," Libby stammered.

"And?" Mrs. Thump asked.

Libby looked at her mother and silently pleaded with her to stop.

Mim and Brittany stood with their mouths open, waiting to see what would happen next.

Libby didn't know what to say. Didn't her mother

understand that Brittany had made her feel like a dork at swim practice? Didn't she see that she was embarrassing her now? Whose side was her mother on, anyway?

Mrs. Thump shook her head and walked away, Brittany and Mim became distracted by a tray of lip gloss that was making the rounds. The awful moment had passed.

But Libby knew her mom was disappointed in her. She thought back to the day before when her mother said that she didn't have to brag or try to be someone that she wasn't. But Libby wasn't so sure . . . maybe she *did* have to be someone that she wasn't.

17

SOMEONE NAMED BRITTANY

That evening there was a silent dinner. Then Libby went straight to her room and stayed there. Margaret sat on Libby's bed and gave her an understanding look.

Libby hugged the dog and Margaret licked Libby's nose. "At least you still like me," Libby said glumly. "I mean, what was I supposed to do?" Margaret flattened her ears and looked concerned. "Was I supposed to say, 'Hey, Brittany? Guess what? I don't even have any riding pants or boots, I didn't ride in any horse show on a champion show jumper.'" Libby sat up and Margaret flopped on her side. "In fact . . . I don't even take riding lessons! In fact . . . I stink at stinkin' swimming and I lie!" Libby fell back on the bed and covered her face with her hands. Margaret stood over Libby and wagged her tail. "It's not funny, Margaret," Libby groaned. Margaret laid down again with a grunt.

"I'm not supposed to brag." Libby pet the dog's head and sighed. "I'm not supposed to try to be something that I'm not. But the thing is, being *me* hasn't been so terrific lately." Margaret's eyes were half closed—she always did that when someone pet her—and Libby thought she might just as well go to sleep too. It had been a horrible day.

Suddenly Libby couldn't wait for it to be morning so that she could escape to High Hopes Horse Farm— the place where she always felt happy.

When Libby woke, she dressed quickly. Laurel was still sleeping and Libby was glad to be on her own. It was beautiful outside, but Libby hardly even noticed as she headed to the barn.

Sal was finishing up the stalls and Emily was in the tack room pulling on her boots. Libby figured she would just slip in, get her grooming equipment, and leave unnoticed to go groom Princess. Libby wanted to be alone to think. But coming toward her down the aisle was Mr. McClave. He moved slower than usual and touched the door of a stall every few feet with one hand to keep his balance.

"Why the long face?" he said.

"I don't know." Libby suddenly felt a little foolish— like maybe she was making a big deal out of nothing.

"You know, that's an old joke." Mr. McClave sat down on a bale of hay to rest, but his eyes twinkled. "It goes like this—a horse walks into a bar and the bartender says, 'Why the long face?'" He laughed at his joke and Libby laughed too.

"So, how's that drawing of General George and me coming along?"

"I haven't started it—but I'm going to, I really am!" Libby said, and decided that it would be the first thing she did when she got back from the barn today.

"Good!" Mr. McClave heaved himself up with some trouble and Libby took his hand. "Because I'm not getting any younger, you know!"

Libby promised Mr. McClave. She felt better and picked up her bucket. But when she turned to leave, Libby stopped dead in her tracks.

Coming toward her in brand-new breeches and boots was somebody she never in a million, billion, trillion years expected to see at High Hopes Horse Farm.

"Hi, Libby," Brittany said.

"What are you doing?" Libby was so shocked she could barely get the words out of her mouth.

"I'm going to take riding lessons!" Brittany said cheerfully.

At each end of the aisle a surreal scene was taking place. At one end Brittany's mother, Suzanne, handed

Sal a check. At the other, Emily led Cough Drop, all tacked up for a lesson.

"Who are you riding?" Libby asked.

"Cough Drop."

"Cough Drop?" Libby dropped her bucket; brushes tumbled out and the bucket rolled a few feet. She couldn't believe it!

It was all she could do not to run out of the barn—but she didn't want anyone to know. She didn't want anyone to know that she was through—through with horses, with riding, with Brittany, and with Sal and Emily. She was through with trying to Live Up to Her Potential, because Libby felt like she had none.

Libby ran the entire way to Princess's shed because she could never be through with her. Princess raised her head and nickered hello, and Libby thought about what Mr. McClave had said that first day: "Sometimes talking to a horse is a whole lot better than talking to another person because horses listen—and they know how you feel."

He was right. "Oh, Princess!" She threw her arms around the horse's neck and cried.

After a while Libby dried her tears and fed the mare her last carrot.

"There's someone named Brittany." Libby hiccuped as she spoke. "If she feeds you a carrot—don't nicker at her when she comes out to visit you, okay? You promise?" Princess nuzzled Libby's neck and Libby rested her face against the mare's cheek. "You be a good girl and don't be lonely." Libby took the horse's face in both hands and looked her straight in the eyes. "I love you," she whispered, and kissed the horse's nose. Then she left.

18
WHAT DO YOU DO?

What do you do when everything in life seems unfair?

When you want to take riding lessons and your stupid sister gets them instead—even though it was your idea in the first place?

When you try to Live Up to Your Potential and then get punished for doing it?

When your stupid sister gets riding boots and you're

forced into going on the swim team even though you stink at swimming?

When you are embarrassed by your mother at a Princess Spa Party that you never wanted to go to in the first place?

When the only thing you want to do you can't because of stupid Just Exactly Like Herself Brittany?

If you are Libby Thump, you stew. At least she had the perfect stewing partner, Margaret. Next to begging for food, stewing was Margaret's specialty. She could lie on a couch, a bed, or the front lawn forever.

She sat with Margaret day after day and stewed.

"Think about it this way," Libby explained to her. "It would be like if another dog suddenly showed up here at our house. Imagine a really cute, perfect little dog, who came when you called her, and didn't eat the covers off paperback books or tear up all the tissues in the wastebaskets, a dog that never threw up on the carpets and did everything that it was told. And Mom and Dad and Laurel—and even I—started to like this dog better than you. Can you imagine how crummy you'd feel?" Margaret stared at Libby with soulful eyes. "That's how I feel." Libby said. Margaret dutifully curled up in a ball and stared off into space because that was how she stewed.

Libby stewed and no one even noticed. Not her sister, her mother, or her father.

Libby knew why—because everybody thought Mrs. Williams was right about her; she did not apply herself, and this was just another example that Libby did not Live Up to Her Potential.

Her thoughts turned to her teacher. Libby wondered if Mrs. Williams had "applied" herself. Could she have been a brain surgeon, or a scientist, or even president of the United States? Or had she taken the easy way out by teaching fourth grade? Had Mrs. Williams lived up to her potential? For that matter, Libby wondered, had her mother? Her father? Was Laurel?

The thing was, how did you know what your

potential was? Libby wasn't sure. But one thing she did know—she could swim till the cows came home and it wouldn't make any difference. She stank at swimming.

Libby quit the swim team.

Her mother sighed. "Well, you can lead a horse to water . . ."

But you can't make him go to swim practice. Libby sighed too. At least she could still draw.

Or could she?

Libby stared at the photo of General George and Mr. McClave. She began to draw but had to throw it out and start again. She hadn't picked up a pencil since the end of school, and her hand felt awkward and unsure. She looked closer at the picture, took a deep breath, and began again—and then several more times after that.

Libby was spending a lot of time working on her drawing from the photo of Mr. McClave. It kept her mind off wondering what she was missing at the

barn. She tried not to pay attention to Laurel or ask any questions about High Hopes Horse Farm. She tried not to think about Brittany taking lessons, riding Cough Drop, and making friends with Emily and Sal. She tried not to think about Princess nickering at Brittany for carrots. And then Laurel came home from the barn with unsettling news. "Mr. McClave got hurt."

"Is he all right?" Libby was upset.

"I don't know—he fell and hit his head," Laurel said.

"And you don't know how badly he's hurt?" Libby's voice trembled.

"I told you, I don't know—he won't be at the barn for a while."

Libby worried about Mr. McClave. Was he going to be all right? What about General George—who was grooming him? Who was feeding him carrots? Who was coming to the barn and talking to him about the good old days?

From there on out Libby did nothing but work on the drawing of Mr. McClave and General George. She was resolved to make it extra special. She studied a crosshatch technique using pen and ink that she liked in a picture book and taught herself how to do it. By the time she had it finished, Libby thought it was the best drawing she had ever done in her entire life!

Every day Libby waited for Laurel to come home from the barn to find out about Mr. McClave.

A week passed and then another, and then at the beginning of the third week Laurel heard that Mr. McClave was better. "I think he might be back at the barn in the next few days."

Libby was relieved, but the next day at the beach, with no swim practice to contend with, she sat stewing on the sand. She wanted to see Mr. McClave—to give him the drawing, because she knew it would make him happy—but Libby would have to go back to the barn to do that. Mim plunked herself down on a towel. She tore open a bag of M&M's and offered some to Libby. "Still haven't been back to the barn?"

"That's over," Libby said. She noticed that Mim's blue nail polish from the manicure at the party had started to chip off.

"Over?" Mim spoke with her mouth full.

"Brittany's taking riding lessons."

"I know, but so what?"

"I just can't." Libby shook her head and ate the candies one at a time. Mim looked concerned but had another session of ballet to get to. Libby watched her friend disappear up the beach and out of view.

Libby walked down by the water. Little kids screamed and played in the surf while seagulls waddled about tamely looking for a stray piece of crust from a sandwich. She stood shin-deep in the ocean as waves pushed and pulled the sand around her feet.

She watched a wave break close to shore and then go out. Tiny shells and pebbles coated the sand, and Libby bent down to pick up an interesting piece of colored glass. It was a deep green and caught the light like an emerald when she held it up to the sun.

Libby wished she could go back to High Hopes more than anything else in the world. So what was stopping her? Was it the thought of seeing Brittany there riding Cough Drop and doing all the things that Libby thought were hers and hers alone? She closed her hand over the shard of green glass and then threw it into the frothy waves.

Libby stepped off the beach now and went to look for Laurel to see if there was any more news about Mr. McClave. She passed rows and rows of gray wood lockers that had been bleached by the sun. There was a smell of salt and creosote in the air, and the gritty feel of sand underfoot that had been tracked up from the beach, but Libby noticed none of it. She smelled horses and hay, and the sweet, grassy breath of Princess; she felt the rutted dried mud of the paddock underfoot. Libby turned the corner, and at the end of the row two figures stood—a boy and a girl. The boy lightly touched the girl's shoulder, her hair floated in the breeze, and then they kissed. Libby ducked back around the corner because the girl was her sister. The girl was Laurel.

That night Laurel came to Libby's room. "I thought you'd want these. . . ."

"Your boots?" Libby's voice rose in surprise.

"Yeah, I'm not going to be needing them. It's almost time to go back to school and there are other things . . ."

Like having a dorky boyfriend, Libby thought, and a disapproving expression unconsciously stole across her face.

"Horses aren't everything, you know, Libby." Laurel handed over the boots and Libby gratefully accepted them. She would not argue the point because in a sense what her sister said was true. To Laurel, horses *weren't* everything. It's just that to Libby, they *were*.

19

BACK TO HIGH HOPES!

L ibby eagerly tried the boots on, and with two pairs
of socks they fit. Now *she* looked like a real rider!
She had to go back to the barn and see Cough Drop,
Sal and Emily, Mr. McClave and General George, and
most of all Princess—she missed them with all her
heart. She couldn't be apart from them another day.

That night when Libby's mother came to her room
to say good night, she sat on the bed. "I need to tell you
something." She put her feet up and leaned on one elbow.

"You know how long Suzanne and I have been friends?"

Libby didn't.

"Since we were your and Brittany's age. We grew up together." Mrs. Thump searched Libby's eyes for a reaction.

Libby said nothing.

"When I go running with Suzanne, she always gets a little bit ahead." To demonstrate, Mrs. Thump held her thumb and her forefinger five inches apart. "Just enough to make me feel like I'm not as fast as she is."

Libby hugged her knees and listened.

"And you know what she does at the end of the run?"

Libby shook her head.

"Vroom!" Mrs. Thump pantomimed a speeding race car with one hand that motioned around a curve and shot out in front of her. "She sprints off, leaving me in the dust."

"Doesn't that make you mad?" Libby asked.

"It used to—it used to make me not want to even run with her. But I surprised myself."

"How?" Libby asked.

"I found out that running with Suzanne was making me a stronger runner."

"But Brittany wouldn't let me on her team—she did it on purpose just so her team would win!" Libby said defensively.

"Libby." Her mother said her name and it was as if Libby were hearing it for the first time. "You have to understand that winning is more important to some people than it is to others."

"Are you saying I don't care about winning—'cause I do!"

"No. I'm saying that winning isn't always the most important thing."

"Then what is?" Libby held her hands up in dismay.

Her mom straightened up and her eyes were bright. "*Trying*—that's the most important thing."

Libby looked down at her feet. "I wouldn't have done that to her, is all."

Mrs. Thump reached forward and smoothed her

daughter's hair. "And that's why I'm so proud of you."

Libby raised her eyes. "You are? You don't wish I was more like Brittany?"

Her mother put her arms around Libby. "Is that what you think?" her mother said, surprised.

Libby shook her head yes.

"I would *never* want you to be like Brittany or anybody else." Her mother kissed her forehead. Libby got under the covers and her mother switched off the light. "Just be you."

In the morning Libby wore her boots down to breakfast and brought with her the drawing that she wanted to give to Mr. McClave.

"Looks just like the picture!" Laurel said, and then went back to her phone.

Mrs. Thump glanced at her husband. "I could *never* do that!"

"Me neither." Mr. Thump squeezed Libby's shoulder and then took his coffee out to his office.

Just as she was leaving for the barn, Libby's father

called to her. "This is for you, Lib." It was an envelope with some money in it. "For your riding lessons."

"Really?" Libby stood in the doorway, unbelieving.

"Your mother and I talked it over."

Libby hugged her father. Then she ran all the way to the park, through the woods, to the railed fence. The pasture spread out before her and glittered with dew. Princess grazed up on the hill under blue skies. A horse so white she almost looked pink. A green carpet of grass rolled away from her in all directions and Libby's heart swelled.

"Princess! Princess!" Libby called. The horse raised her head and whinnied. Libby raced across the field, her braids lashing behind her. They both reached the shed at the same time. Princess whirled around and snorted.

"I've got to see Sal right away, girl," Libby cried, and climbed quickly through the rail fence of the paddock. "I'll be back—I've got so much to tell you!"

Libby held tightly to the cardboard covering that she had carefully placed her drawing in. As she made her way to the barn, she could see that there had been changes at High Hopes Horse Farm. A Dumpster sat in the weeds, and some workmen pulled the rusted, ancient farm equipment out of tangled grass, while others threw junk into the receptacle.

Inside, cobwebs had been swept out. The doors and windows had been opened and the barn was flooded with light. Libby burst into the tack room to leave her drawing until Mr. McClave showed up. She was surprised to see that all the tack was clean. Out front a few kids in jodhpurs and low boots sat on the mounting block, talking and laughing, waiting for riding lessons.

"Hi, stranger!" Emily had Cough Drop in the aisle and was tacking him up. Libby waved and called hello before she dashed out to the ring to see Sal.

"Sal!" Libby shouted.

Sal was in the middle of the ring. Three students trotted happily around him on Summer and on a horse and pony Libby had never seen. Sal turned and gave her a big smile.

"Sal!" Libby called breathlessly again, and waved the envelope. "I've got money for lessons now! See?"

"That's great, Libby." Sal walked over to her. "Thing is, though, Cough Drop's all booked up now."

"Booked up?" Libby's face began to fall. "Well, what about Summer—I could ride her."

"She's booked up too. Libby, you've been gone awhile and I've got lots of lessons—I'll have to see."

"See? See when?" Libby was bewildered.

Sal went back to his students, and Libby left the ring. She had the money to take lessons, but now Sal was busy—too busy for her—and she didn't blame him. She *had* been gone awhile—home stewing. Now she wouldn't get to ride and it was her own fault.

Back in the barn, with her riding helmet under her arm, Brittany waited for her lesson on Cough Drop.

"Hi, Brittany," Libby said sadly.

"Sorry about the party," Brittany said to Libby sheepishly.

"What do you mean?" Libby stiffened.

Brittany looked up at the rafters. "I was so embarrassed I wanted to crawl into a hole."

"Why?" Libby's mind was racing.

"All that princess stuff?" Brittany laughed self-consciously.

"My mom was really into it," Libby said, grateful that Brittany hadn't brought up the awkward moment when her mother tried to get her to fess up.

"Mine *too*—she thinks I'm still, like, three years old." Brittany rolled her eyes and shifted her helmet to the other arm. There was an uncomfortable silence until Brittany spoke. "Can I ask you something?"

Libby nodded.

"Did your mom have a fit when you quit the swim team?"

Libby wrinkled her nose. "Kind of—why?"

Brittany took a deep breath. "Because I want to quit."

"You do?" Libby hadn't expected that. "Why?"

"Because I can't beat those new girls—they're so

much faster than me." Brittany looked away.

For the first time Libby started to think that maybe she and Brittany had more in common than she had ever thought. "Don't quit," Libby said.

"You did," Brittany said matter-of-factly.

Then Libby almost couldn't believe what she heard herself say next. "I'm going back to swim practice."

"You are? Why?" Brittany's eyes were wide.

"Maybe I'm not as bad at swimming as I think I am," Libby said. "But I'll never know if I don't try." She shrugged. "Who knows? I might surprise myself."

"Maybe we both will." Brittany held out her hand. "Shake?"

Libby took Brittany's hand. "Shake."

Emily led Cough Drop down the aisle. Brittany got on the pony at the mounting block and walked into the ring.

Libby stood at the rail and watched Brittany's lesson.

Dust swirled around the ring as the horses circled.

Libby rested her chin on her hands and listened to Sal instructing. She closed her eyes and pretended she was riding. She could feel the tension from her hands and forearms and shoulders to the horse's mouth. The pressure against her legs as she drove the horse forward. She was turning, and cantering, jumping high fences, galloping through open fields.

"Libby!" Emily was talking to her.

Libby turned, and there was Emily holding Princess, who was wearing a bridle and a saddle.

"Princess!" Libby gasped. The horse stretched her neck toward Libby, looking for treats, and Libby rubbed her face.

Brittany and the other kids watched from the middle of the ring.

Sal came over and Emily handed him a riding helmet.

Libby couldn't take her eyes off Princess. It was astonishing how she looked now—exactly as if the photos from the tack room had come to life! "I can't wait to see you ride her, Sal!"

"Not going to ride her," Sal said nonchalantly.

"You're not?" Libby didn't understand.

"Nope." Sal placed the helmet on Libby's head. "You are."

"Me? I'm riding Princess?" Libby squeaked. "For real?"

"For real," Sal said. He gave her a leg up and adjusted her stirrups. Libby walked next to the rail, grinning from ear to ear while Sal told her to turn and halt, to half circle and trot, to change direction, and circle again. Libby trotted around the ring on Princess and realized something incredible had happened over the summer without her even knowing.

She hadn't taken a single lesson, but somehow, some way, Libby Thump was learning to ride!

20

BLUE SKIES

Libby couldn't believe how lucky she really was. Sal told her that as long as the mare wasn't jumped or ridden hard, maybe the exercise would do her good. From now on Libby could ride Princess!

Libby led her into the barn, and Emily helped her take off the saddle and bridle and put on the halter. She was about to lead Princess outside to wash off her back when she looked down the aisle and there was Mr. McClave. He was using a walker.

"Mr. McClave!" Libby shouted, and ran to him. "Are you okay?"

He looked a bit thinner and moved a little slower but was otherwise the same in his pressed jeans, low brown hacking boots, and short-sleeved golf shirt. "I'm fine," he said gruffly. "Except for this ridiculous contraption!"

"But it helps you to walk, right?" Libby looked up into his face with concern.

"I suppose." The old man laughed in spite of himself.

"I have something for you—wait right here!" Libby ran off to the tack room. She appeared a moment later with the drawing.

"Look!" Libby held the drawing for him to see.

He studied it for a long time, then said, "It's marvelous! Wait till George sees this!"

Libby said shyly, "I want you to have it to remember the good old days."

"I will treasure it always, my dear," Mr. McClave said. He took Libby's hand and kissed it.

Suddenly there was a loud banging noise that came

from the end of the aisle. *Bang! Bang! Bang!*

"It's my first day back," Mr. McClave said. "George is anxious to see me!"

General George kicked at his stall door. His neck was arched and he bobbed his gigantic head up and down. He seemed to have grown twenty years younger. *Bang! Bang! Bang!* He kicked at the door, trying to get to Mr. McClave.

Mr. McClave called to him, "I'm coming, George—settle down."

But Mr. McClave was slow and George wouldn't settle down. The old man stopped to catch his breath and George became even more agitated. He reared and wheeled around in his stall, whinnying loudly.

"Here, let me help you." Libby took hold of Mr. McClave's arm.

"Easy! Easy!" Mr. McClave called out to George.

But George leaned all his weight against the door, which bowed out alarmingly.

"Sal!" Libby screamed. "Emily!"

The horse's black eyes were fixed on Mr. McClave as he pushed with all his might. Emily came running and so did Sal, but it was too late!

CRASH! The door burst off its runner. General George came trotting down the aisle, completely oblivious to the door hanging around his massive neck like a yoke. *Clip, clop! Clip, clop!* He smelled Mr. McClave's face and shoulders and chest as if to make sure for himself that his old friend was all right.

Sal and Emily immediately lifted the door off the horse. "He missed you!" Sal laughed.

"I missed him, too." Mr. McClave took a handkerchief out of his back pocket and wiped his eyes. "There now," he said softly to the horse, and patted his neck. "I didn't leave you. I'm here, I'm here."

Libby turned to go and could hear Mr. McClave talking to his horse as he showed him the drawing. "Remember that day? We jumped the five-rail, and the wind blew—but there were blue skies. Remember? Nothing but blue skies."

Libby went to Princess, who had been waiting quietly all this time. Sal stood by the mare and combed her mane over with his fingers. "I guess you have a new rider now, old girl," he said in a soft voice and unclipped the horse from the cross-ties. "But you ought to know that Libby's very persistent—that means she never gives up"—Sal smiled warmly at Libby—"on horses . . . *or* people."

He handed Libby the lead rope and together they walked out of the barn into the sunshine. Libby watched him head back to the dusty ring to teach another lesson. She gazed off into the distance, out to the pasture where she had first seen the big white mare up on the hill. Princess rested her head on Libby's shoulder and Libby stroked her nose with one hand.

No, she wasn't the Best Rider in the Entire World, just like Emily. She was just Libby Thump, riding Princess, and for now that was all right.

"Blue skies," she whispered, and Libby knew that Princess was listening.

Here's a sneak peek at the next book in the Libby
of High Hopes series, where Libby has to ride
Saddleshoes—the most difficult horse
in High Hopes Horse Farm.
How will she ever win a blue ribbon
and help the farm?

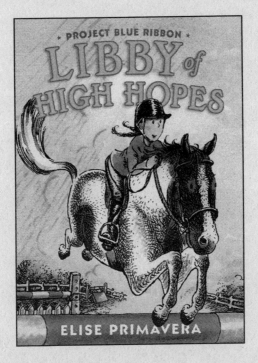

LIBBY THE RIDER

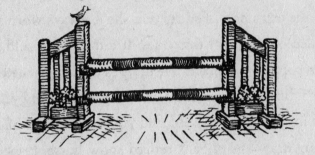

Libby Thump wished for a blue ribbon. A satin royal blue ribbon with a rosette and the words "First Place" written in gold lettering. There was going to be a horse show in three weeks and that's exactly where she hoped to win one. Libby was excited because Sal, who owned High Hopes Horse Farm, was supposed to tell her today if he thought she was ready to ride in the show.

She sat on the floor of her bedroom trying to pull

on her left boot. "Come on," she said impatiently, but it wouldn't budge. She'd grown an inch since last summer and the riding boots that had been handed down from her sister were beginning to get tight. She yanked off the extra pair of socks that she'd always worn and pulled on a pair of thin ones. It did the trick and her foot slipped into place. She jumped up and reached for her riding helmet, when something caught her eye.

Libby tilted her head and squinted at one of the many drawings of Sal's retired show horse, Princess, she'd taped to the wall. She suddenly noticed for the first time there was something wrong with the way she'd drawn the white mare and grabbed an eraser and pencil off her table to fix it.

"*Libbyyyyyyyyy!*" her mother called to her. "Please walk the dog!"

"In a minute!" Libby called back. Margaret gazed up at her and wagged her tail expectantly. Libby got the leash—the drawing would have to wait—but as she turned to leave she caught a reflection of herself in the mirror. There were the same long dark braids, dark eyes, and oval face, but in her boots and jeans and quilted vest she looked like a real rider! Libby wondered what her fourth-grade teacher from last year would think of her now. Libby remembered what Mrs. Williams had written on Libby's report card the last day of school.

Libby needs to apply herself. Sometimes she does not pay attention or follow directions as well as she should. Libby needs to live up to her potential!

Back then Libby wasn't even sure what potential was. By now she had memorized the meaning of the word: "something that can develop or become actual." Libby knew just what that "something" was, too; she was a rider! It was what she was meant to be. She just hoped that she had the potential to someday become a really good rider. She thought she could feel it in there, just itching to get out!

Sure enough, a lot had changed since Mrs. Williams's class. Throughout the fall and all winter Libby had been riding Princess, and she was even learning to jump.

Libby moved her face closer to the mirror. She sucked in her cheeks and tried to imagine what she would look like when she was grown up. Would she be a really good rider by then? Did she have what it would take?

"*Libbyyyyy!*" her mother called again.

Libby glanced at the clock on her night table. "Oh my gosh!" she cried, and raced out of the room with Margaret scrambling behind her. "Laurel! Laurel!" Libby pressed the leash into her sister's hands. "I've got a lesson—I don't want to be late—just this once, please? Thanks!"

Libby tore out of the house. Her sister stamped her foot and yelled, "*Libbyyyyyy!*"

Libby pretended she didn't hear and ran as fast as she could through the park to the path in the woods. She never stopped till she stood in the grassy field on top of the same hill as in the pictures that she'd covered her bedroom walls with. "Princess! Come on, girl!"

Below the horse nickered and soon there was a

thunder of hooves. The white mare's mane whipped in the wind as she galloped up to meet the girl. She skidded to a stop and nudged Libby's pocket for a carrot.

Libby jogged down the hill and Princess followed behind like an enormous dog. There was the smell of damp earth and new grass. All winter Libby had been looking forward to spring and now it was finally here. She breathed in deeply and sighed. The sky was blue and the air was just beginning to have the first hint of warmth.

At the gate she grabbed the halter and slipped it over the mare's nose. "This has to be our best lesson yet, Princess!" Libby knew that she would have to ride extra-specially well this day in order for Sal to think that she was good enough to compete in the horse show.

As soon as they entered the barn Brittany poked her head out of a stall where she was tacking up Summer, the horse she always rode. Libby's and Brittany's moms were best friends and that had automatically made Libby and Brittany best friends since they were babies. They'd had a "misunderstanding" last year, but now Libby was glad they were best friends again.

"Lesson today?" Brittany asked.

"Yep!" Libby grinned as she passed.

At the end of the aisle was one of Sal's boarders, Mr. McClave and his horse, General George. "Hi, Mr. McClave!" Libby shouted.

The old man paused from brushing off his horse. "All ready for your lesson?"

"All ready!" Libby answered, and secured Princess to the cross ties. She hurried to the tack room.

A blond curly-haired woman in jeans and hacking boots bustled down the aisle with several flakes of hay that she threw into stalls. Emily was Sal's wife and helped him run the stable.

"Hi, Emily!" Libby called to her.

"Libby!" Emily called back. "Sal will be right out!"

"Great!" Libby grabbed her saddle and bridle and felt the butterflies in her stomach that were always there right before she was to have a jumping lesson. She still couldn't pass by the photos in the tack room of Sal riding the big white horse over the gigantic fences without getting goose bumps. Now here she was, Libby Thump, jumping Princess herself.

She was so anxious to get out to the ring that it was all she could do to take the time to pick out each of the mare's hooves and then brush her off and tack her up. Libby's fingers nervously fumbled with the snaps on her riding helmet. All ready, she led Princess down the aisle.

She wanted everything to go well this afternoon.

Brittany poked her head out of Summer's stall again, "Watch out for Saddleshoes!"

"Oh no!" Libby groaned.

"Oh yes!" Brittany said.

Outside Libby could see that Brittany was right. There was Saddleshoes. With his dazzling white legs, brown spots on his neck and rump, and a handsome blaze down the front of his face Saddleshoes was the best-looking pony around. But . . . as far as Libby was concerned he was also the worst pony there ever was.

Libby entered the ring careful to steer Princess far away from him, for he could deliver a mean kick. Suddenly there was a gust of wind and Saddleshoes spooked to the side. Somewhere the sound of a tractor started up and he shied and tried to buck.

His rider, Kate, was eighteen and small for her age, which was why she was still able to ride a large pony. She was also a talented and fearless rider and the only one who could control Saddleshoes.

Throughout all of the pony's shenanigans Princess remained quiet and steady. She paid absolutely no attention to Saddleshoes when he flattened his ears at her.

Kate gathered her reins and headed him toward a fence. Libby walked Princess around to the far corner of the ring to get out of the way. The spotted pony leaped off at a ferocious speed. Libby could barely look. Kate tried to hold him. He raised his head and fought her with every stride but somehow he met the

fence perfectly. He could jump beautifully, but Libby knew that before Kate bought the pony from Sal, when other kids rode Saddleshoes, it was a completely different story. He would rush his fences only to slam on the brakes at the last minute. A "dirty stop," Sal called it, because the pony did it so quickly and for no reason.

"Good boy!" Kate praised him, and leaned over to pat his neck.

Libby frowned. So far this afternoon was not going at all the way she'd wanted it to. She could just see stupid Saddleshoes charging right in front of Princess as they tried to jump a fence, or worse, kick her if she got too close—you just never knew with that pony. He was unpredictable. Libby looked around for Sal and hoped that he would make them leave, when she noticed a lone girl leaning on the fence. She was standing next to a short, squat, dark-haired woman—probably the girl's mother. There were always kids—mostly girls—hanging around the barn, but Libby had never seen this girl before. She had a solemn, oblong face, long poker-straight light brown Alice in Wonderland hair with bangs across her high forehead. The girl's stern expression reminded Libby of the kind she'd seen on adults right before they were about to tell her not to do something.

As Libby went by, the girl said, "I like your horse," in a surprisingly shy tone of voice.

"Thanks, but she's not mine," Libby replied.

Kate and Saddleshoes jumped over another fence and Libby held her breath. It made her so nervous to watch him. He went for Kate because she was a fantastic rider, but he stopped or tried to run away with every other kid Libby had ever seen try to ride him. She didn't know why he was so bad. All Libby knew was that she was glad *she* didn't have to ride him. Libby wished again that Kate and Saddleshoes would leave the ring. She didn't want them to ruin her jumping lesson today of all days.

What Libby didn't know was that one of her worst fears was about to come true.

Look for
Libby of High Hopes: Project Blue Ribbon
at your bookstore or local library
to read the rest of Libby's story.

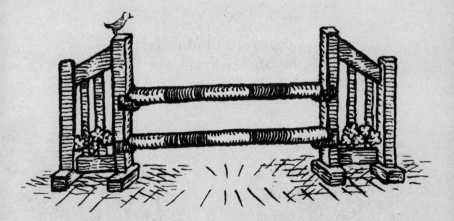

Did you LOVE reading this book?

Visit the Whyville...

Where you can:

- Discover great books!
- Meet new friends!
- Read exclusive sneak peeks and more!

Log on to visit now!

bookhive.whyville.net